WHISPER LAKE

JAMES MELZER

FIRST EDITION
ISBN 978-0615816302
10 9 8 7 6 5 4 3 2 1

For Jenny

ONE

Trevor reached out his hand and turned down the stereo in the minivan. He cocked an eyebrow at his girlfriend, Sarah, sitting next to him in the passenger seat. "Wait, are you seriously telling me that women are better drivers than men? Seriously?"

"Seriously." She snapped her gum and smiled.

He scoffed and shook his head. He didn't care how good she looked wearing nothing but a bikini top and cutoff jean shorts, her bare feet propped up on the dash. She wasn't going to win this argument.

"Kincaid," he said, glancing over his shoulder at the back seat, "help me out here, would you."

"Yo, I know for a fact that men are better drivers than women."

"Oh yeah? How?" Amy asked, intrigued by where this was all going.

Kincaid looked at the girl sitting next to him and patted her on her knee. She was also wearing shorts, though hers were a bit more modest than Sarah's and at least had the decency to cover her thighs.

Kincaid counted on his fingers, saying, "Because when I was ten, my mom got in a car accident, and when I was fifteen, my sister got in a car accident. Then, when I was sixteen, my aunt was in a car accident."

"So?" Sarah said. "That doesn't prove anything."

"Sure it does."

"How?"

"You want to know how many accidents my dad has been in? Zero. You want to know how many accidents I've been in? Zero? My brother? Same thing. No accidents."

"So statistically speaking," Trevor chimed in, "women are *worse* drivers than men."

"Right," Kincaid agreed, reaching into the back of the minivan to find a soda.

"Grab me one of those, would you?" Amy asked.

He nodded and passed her a can.

As if proving his point, Trevor grinned at Sarah and cranked the stereo once again. She rolled her eyes and stared out the passenger side window, watching the country scenery pass them by.

The four of them had been bickering back and forth for hours like a bunch of high school kids. Even though they had graduated a month earlier and knew better, they just couldn't help themselves. Some habits died hard.

Trevor drummed his thin fingers on the steering wheel, already forgetting about what they were arguing over. He was in too good a mood to dwell on the negative. This was his last summer of freedom. The last for all of them, really. Though they still had their whole lives ahead of them, each of them were heading off to college in the fall and this trip was the perfect opportunity to cut loose one more time and really enjoy it for all it was worth before they had to step into adulthood.

Trevor glanced at the digital clock. They were still an hour away from his grandmother's cabin, the one he had been tasked with cleaning so his parents could put it on the market. A simple job: just go up and spend the week cleaning it out and be back by next Sunday night. His mother wanted nothing more to do with it, though he had no idea why. All she told him was to keep the pictures and junk the rest. His father would go up with a trash removal company at a later date to take away all the furniture. All he had to do was get it sparkling clean for prospective buyers.

At first they weren't going to let him take any friends with him, but after a little convincing they could all handle themselves, Trevor's parents caved and agreed to let him take Amy, Sarah, and Kincaid. After all, they had managed to stay out of trouble together for most of high school, and who knew how long they'd have left before they all lost contact with one another and started their own lives? People come in and out of your life so fast at that age, so they didn't see any harm in it. As long as there was no drinking.

"We got enough beer, right?" Sarah asked.

"You bet," Kincaid said.

"That fake ID your brother gave you was a godsend, man," Trevor yelled over the music.

Amy reached into her purse and pulled out a bag of weed. "We got enough of this, too," she laughed.

"Awe yeah, that's what I'm talking about." Kincaid tried to snatch it from her but she was too quick.

"Not yet, mister," she leaned over and offered him her lips instead. He gladly accepted them.

"Hey, hey, hey," Trevor looked at them in the rearview. "Save it for the cabin."

He winked at Sarah. She pulled down one side of her bikini top and flashed him her breast.

Trevor swerved the minivan onto the shoulder.

"Better drivers, huh?" she laughed.

"You too," he grinned at her.

She chomped her teeth at him, rolled down her window, and shouted into the breeze.

Yes sir, it was going to be one fine summer, even though the circumstances surrounding their trip were somewhat grim.

His only remaining grandparent, Trevor's grandmother had passed away three months earlier. Thankfully, it had been peaceful. She went in her sleep. His mother had been pretty broken up about it, of course—it was *her* mother. Trevor remained indifferent, though. He had never really been close to her growing up, only spending Christmases with her and the occasional Thanksgiving. His grandfather had passed away when he was little, and his fathers' parents were dead before he was born, so he never knew them.

He thought it might feel weird, going through a dead woman's things. Especially knowing the cabin was her sanctuary. Who knew what he would find up there?

Granddad built it for her a long time ago as a place for her to call her own. She would go there for a couple of weeks in the summer each year to get away from it all. *To recharge,* as Trevor's mother put it, though he never understood what she needed to recharge from. His grandparents had money, so it wasn't like they had suffered for anything.

"A woman needs a place all her own," his mother said to him one day.

Trevor was quick to point out that *she* didn't have any place to call her own.

"But I do. When I shut that door and turn up the music in the spare bedroom, it's like there's no one else around. It's just me and my paintings. Your father knew that, that's why he gave it to me rather than put his exercise equipment in there. Your grandfather knew it, too."

Trevor had just nodded and fixed himself a sandwich.

He'd never figure out women. Even Sarah was a bit of a mystery to him.

She sure as hell smelled good, though.

They had been on and off again since eighth grade, but this last year had been different. He didn't know if it was because they were growing older or what, but they seemed to be as serious as they'd ever been. Even the 'M' word had been brought up a couple of times, though Trevor didn't know if he was ready to make that leap yet. Marriage was, well, it was forever. Or at least until you got sick of the person and found yourself in court with your belongings split down the middle.

Kincaid and Amy were a little different. They had only been together a few months, but they had known each other for years. They were still in that lovey-dovey early stage of a relationship. Always sneaking off to make-out any chance they got. Trevor swore one day Amy was going to turn up pregnant, but Kincaid assured him that he always—always—pulled out at just the right moment.

He checked the gas gauge. They were fine for now but he'd definitely have to fill up before they returned home or else they would find themselves stranded on the side of the road in the middle of nowhere.

"So what's this place called again?" Sarah asked him.

Trevor turned down the music, but not all the way. It played softly in the background as he spoke.

"Whisper Lake."

"Sounds peaceful."

"As far as I know it is. Apparently the cabin is literally in the middle of nowhere. No neighbors, no stores. Nothing. There's not even a landline there and cell phones? Forget about it, so I hope no one planned on surfing for porn while we were there," he glanced at Kincaid.

"Hey, that was one time, man. One time."

"Yeah, and besides," Amy purred, "he doesn't need porn."

The two locked lips once again and Trevor sighed.

"It never stops with those two."

Sarah leaned over and reached between his legs. He did his best to keep control of the minivan but ended up swerving once more, this time into the opposite lane. He was rounding a corner and narrowly avoided a head on collision with a Prius. A horn blared loudly at him and he corrected the steering.

"Jesus, Sarah."

"What?" she blinked and bit her bottom lip. "I didn't do anything."

His mouth curled up into a sly grin. How could he stay mad at someone who just wanted to jump his bones?

"Come on, we're almost there. Let's just cool it until tonight, okay?"

"Okay, Daddy," she cooed.

"Oh, man," he chuckled. "You're something else, you know that?"

He wanted nothing more than to stop the vehicle and fuck her brains out right then and there, but he had to control himself. If Amy and Kincaid weren't around, maybe, but for the moment he thought about something other than Sarah's lips wrapped around his shaft, and let the bulge in his pants subside.

Grandma.

Nothing less sexual than that.

From what he remembered she was a quiet woman. Never bothering anyone with trivial matters or getting caught up in local gossip. She wasn't like the other old ladies he knew who liked to sit around all day and act like hens in a coop, constantly squawking about this one and that. She was different. Kept to herself, and only said what needed to be said.

When she spoke, people listened because it was something she didn't do often.

Completely the opposite of his mother, who gabbed with her friends day in and day out about the neighbors.

He frowned at the thought and put her out of his mind, paying attention to the road instead.

Bushes turned to trees as they drove deeper into the country, and the woods.

Whisper Lake wasn't exactly what you'd call a tourist destination. It was nothing more than a small body of water surrounded by foliage as thick as thieves. His mother told him the cabin was on the north side, and it wouldn't be hard to spot. It was the only one around for miles. There had been others at one time, but now they were all gone. Abandoned or torn down; left to rot along with the rest of the economy.

Still, he had the directions etched in his mind should he need them, but from the way she described it he didn't think they'd be necessary.

To the delight of everyone else he turned up the music and they drove the rest of the way conversation-free until he came upon a dirt road off to his right. It was barely noticeable in the thick woods but Sarah had been the one to spot it and call out to him.

"That must be the place," he said, steering onto it.

The minivan bumped and rocked like a carnival ride as he reduced its speed. The last thing he needed was for a tire to blow out.

"How far down?" Amy asked.

"About three miles."

"Good, cause I gotta take a piss," Kincaid added, "and this rough terrain isn't exactly helping my bladder any."

"Hang on, hang on. We're almost there."

Trevor slowed the minivan to a crawl as the trees parted and a patch of land gave way on his left to a clearing.

Everyone turned to face the wide-open space. Amy rolled down her window and Kincaid leaned over her to get a better look. She slapped him on the forehead.

Sarah put her chin on Trevor's shoulder. "There it is," she whispered.

The cabin came into view.

It was a spacious bungalow with two bedrooms, a kitchen, living room area, and a porch on the far side that overlooked the lake, which licked the edge of it. Granddad had gone all out when he built the place, and everything looked fine from where they were sitting.

Except for one thing.

"Uh, Trev?" Kincaid asked. "I thought you said your grandmother was dead?"

The lights were on and the front door was wide open.

"She is.

He parked, killed the engine, and they all sat quietly looking at the cabin that was supposed to be void of any human life.

TWO

"Hello?" Trevor tapped on the open door and stuck his head in, hoping to hell it wouldn't be lopped off by some deranged killer.

Kincaid, Amy, and Sarah huddled close together behind him.

He stopped short and they ran into his back.

"Geez, guys. A little room."

He was more curious than anything to find out what was going on. As far as he knew no one else was supposed to be there. The cabin had been sitting empty for over a year. His grandmother hadn't returned since last May, and died before she got a chance to come back.

He sniffed the air and winced.

"Holy hell."

"What's that stench?"

"I don't know."

They passed the threshold when no one answered his call.

A long hall stretched out before them leading into the living room. To the left were the bathroom and two bedrooms, and off to the right and around a corner was the kitchen. There was a floor mat just past the door with muddy footprints on it, and a closet next to that.

Trevor opened it slowly. No coats.

"This is too weird," Amy whispered.

Kincaid lifted his eyebrows, agreeing with her.

"Hello?" Trevor called out again.

Nothing.

The further they got into the cabin, the worse the stench became.

He pulled his shirt up over his nose and rounded the corner into the kitchen. The others were still well behind him checking out the muddy mat, so they didn't see what he saw.

"Oh fuck."

Four dead rabbits hung from hooks embedded in the ceiling, split and gutted. On the long counter his grandfather had built with his bare hands was the carcass of a deer, waiting to be skinned. Its dead eyes stared back at him and Trevor noticed one of its hind legs was mangled and dripping blood. Flies buzzed about, eager to get a piece of it.

Instruments littered the remainder of the kitchen. Knives, mostly, but he caught a glimpse of a couple of bone saws and some small animal traps before he had to turn away.

Amy rounded the corner first and screamed. She covered her mouth and ran back outside to throw up.

Sarah and Kincaid came next and were stunned by the gruesome scene.

"Jesus Christ," Kincaid said.

Sarah's bottom lip quivered and Trevor reached for her, shielding her eyes.

"Don't look, baby."

She sobbed into his shirt.

Trevor glanced at Kincaid and motioned for him to go and tend to Amy. He nodded and backpedaled out of view of the kitchen before turning around and going outside to be with her.

"Who would do such a thing?" Sarah questioned.

Trevor shook his head. "I don't know."

He glanced further into the cabin, half expecting someone to come out and greet them. He didn't know what he'd do if they did, but he was seriously pissed off that someone would defile his grandmother's hideaway like that.

"Wait here," he told Sarah. "I'll be right back."

"Don't go," she grabbed his arm.

He looked into her eyes. Her pupils were wide and terrified but he had to go. He had to know for sure.

He dipped into the kitchen, looked again at the dead deer, and grabbed a gore-stained knife. He held it up to Sarah as if to show her he would be fine. He had protection.

"Stay here."

She grasped for him but he ignored her touch and went in search of whomever it was that had balls big enough to do such a thing.

The bathroom was empty and so was the first bedroom. He looked at the floor and saw more mud trailing into the second bedroom, off to the right of the living room. He looked around in the big room first and saw an ashtray full of cigarette butts.

His grandmother never smoked a day in her life.

Behind him he could hear Amy retching outside still, with Kincaid quietly trying to calm her nerves. *It's better than silence*, he thought.

The second bedroom door was closed and he approached it with care, raising the knife and placing his ear to the grain. He listened for something—anything—that would tell him someone was in there, but there was no noise coming from behind it that he could hear.

He grasped the handle, squeezed it tight, and in one smooth motion turned it and threw open the door.

"All right, asshole," he bellowed.

Emptiness.

The light was on but no one was in there.

He looked at the bed. It was a complete mess. Sheets were strewn about all over it as if it hadn't been made in months, but it was obvious *someone* had been using it. There was a dirty lumberjack shirt on the floor along with bloody, discarded bandages next to it. Trevor inspected the mess.

The bandages were dirty and stained yellow with puss and brown with dried blood. The stench wasn't as bad as the kitchen but the aroma emanating from them still caused bile to rise up into his throat. He choked it back and coughed. Somehow it seemed worse knowing it had come from a human being rather than an animal.

He inspected the closet. Some of grandma's clothes were still hanging in there, and there were three pairs of shoes lying on the ground underneath them that belonged to a woman: two pairs of sandals and a grey pair of runners.

No men's shoes to speak of.

Satisfied the cabin was empty, Trevor went back out into the living room and looked down the hall toward the kitchen. Sarah was nowhere to be seen and he was instantly filled with a sense of panic. Thinking the worst—that someone had come and taken her when he wasn't looking—he ran back down the hallway and out the front door.

No one was outside, either.

"Sarah! Amy!"

"Over here," Kincaid called.

Trevor breathed a sigh of relief when he heard his friend's voice and went around to the other side of the cabin. They were on the deck that overlooked Whisper Lake, sitting on the dry wood.

Amy glanced at the knife still in his hand and felt suddenly sick again.

He threw it in the lake and went to hug Sarah.

"What's going on?" she asked, holding him tight.

Her breasts pushed up against him and any other time that would have given him an instant hard on, but now they just felt comforting against his chest. Warm.

"I don't know, but whoever was here is gone now."

"But what if they come back?" Amy sobbed.

Trevor didn't have an answer for that.

He looked out over the lake and then to his right, into the deep woods. Was it possible someone was out there? Heard them coming and made a run for it? He shuddered at the thought. Someone had to be close by. That deer carcass was fresh.

"You think it's squatters?"

He looked at Kincaid and pulled away from Sarah, softly rubbing her shoulder.

"Could be," he said. "This place has been empty for a long time. Maybe they thought no one was coming back for it. My mom said that's happened a lot up here."

"But your grandmother's stuff is still in there."

"Who knows how these people think," he replied, feeling the onset of a headache.

"What should we do?" Amy got to her feet and put her arm around Kincaid. "Go home?"

"No way. My parents gave me specific orders and if they see this cabin in the shape it is now, they'll flip. Somehow turn it into my fault."

"Well there's no way I'm staying in there with it like that," Sarah folder her arms across her chest and stared daggers into her boyfriend.

He looked her up and down, wanting so badly to be naked with her. God, how could he think of such things at a time like this?

Because I have a dick, that's why.

"What do you say, Kincaid?"

Kincaid frowned at him and kicked a pebble lying on the deck. It plopped into the lake, causing the calm water to ripple some. "You serious?"

Trevor nodded.

"What?"

He looked at Amy and sighed. "He wants me to help him clean it."

"We brought enough supplies that we can take care of that mess and still have plenty left over to do the rest of the cabin the way my parents want it. We'll leave the windows and doors open to air it out and light some candles. We still have a few hours of daylight left so I bet we can clean out that shit before nightfall, and we can do the rest of the place tomorrow."

Sarah and Amy exchanged glances, rolling their eyes at one another.

"Do we have a choice?" Sarah mumbled.

"Not really. Sorry."

"Let's get started then," Kincaid headed for the minivan to get out the floor cleaner, mops, scrub brushes, and bleach they had brought with them.

Trevor wrapped his arms around Sarah one more time and stroked her long, auburn hair. "It'll be okay, babes."

"Promise?"

"Promise."

He kissed her and went to help Kincaid.

He honestly didn't know if it would be okay or not. He had never cleaned up dead animals before. Maybe the stench would be gone, and maybe it wouldn't, but they had to try.

He wasn't kidding about staying. Despite all he had discovered thus far, he wasn't going to let a bunch of squatters keep him from doing the job his folks had tasked him with. Besides, judging from just the single set of footprints, there looked to be only one of them, and he and his friends were four. Plus, they had all the hardware now. Knives, saws; they could protect themselves if they had to.

His anger subsided as his mind switched to the job in front of him while he helped Kincaid grab a bunch of stuff from the van and take it inside the cabin. They set it all just outside the kitchen and looked at the deer carcass.

"That thing's going to be heavy," he said.

Kincaid agreed. "This is some seriously fucked up shit, you know that right?"

"Yeah, I know."

"The girls are really freaked out."

He nodded. "Can you keep a secret?"

"Yeah."

"So am I."

"Good. I'm not the only one."

Trevor snapped on some rubber gloves and handed another pair to his buddy.

"Bend over," he said.

Kincaid put them on and together they stood on either side of the deer. Trevor bumped his head on one of the hanging rabbits and batted it away like he was caught in a spider's web.

"Son of a bitch."

"Come on," Kincaid said, grabbing hold of the dead animals' neck.

Trevor got on the opposite end and wrapped his arms around its lower belly.

"We'll put it on the floor and drag it out, okay?"

"Okay."

"One...two...three."

They lifted as one and grunted at the weight of the seven-point buck. Damn thing had to have been one seventy-five at least. Bending at the knees they lowered it to the ground and gasped when they let it drop.

"Fucking thing stinks to all hell," Trevor moaned, wiping his nose with his forearm.

"We're halfway there, man. Let's not stop now."

Trevor grabbed it by its hind hooves and lifted them off the ground, swinging it around so his back was facing the door. He went slowly in reverse and Kincaid pushed at the head, taking some of the pressure off and giving him better leverage. They got it outside problem free.

"Where should we put it?"

"The lake."

"Seriously?"

"Well, we can put it at the edge of the woods and let a bear take care of it later."

Kincaid thought about that proposal for a moment. He didn't exactly like the idea of a bear hanging around. The thought of something, or someone, else out there was bad enough.

"Lake's good."

"Close your eyes girls, we're coming through."

They dragged it down the porch and to the deck, leaving a bloody trail of dirt behind them.

Sarah and Amy didn't take Trevor's advice and watched as they got the deer in position.

"Make sure it goes out far," Sarah said.

"We'll do our best," Trevor grunted, getting ready to lift it again.

He and Kincaid got it up, swung it three times, and chucked the animal into the water. It landed with a splash and a deep thud, hitting the lake's floor. The water was too shallow and it barely covered the carcass.

"So much for swimming," Amy said.

Trevor went to hug Sarah but she shied away from him.

"Not with those things on," she said, pointing at his rubber gloves. There was dirt and grime on them from the deer's body, and some of it had gotten on his shirt as well.

"Oh. Right," he said, brushing himself off, but that only made it worse. "Come on, man. Let's get this done."

Kincaid pecked Amy on the cheek and they went back inside to take down the rabbits and clean up the blood.

THREE

He watched them from the woods; his large frame crouched behind a thick tree, peeking around it as they threw his deer into the water. The deer he had caught all by himself just by chance after it had snared itself in one of his traps and he broke its neck clean, finishing the job.

His one good eye widened and inside his chest his heart thumped fast and his blood pressure began to rise. The man remained still and silent. There was nothing he could do.

Yet.

A branch brushed against his forehead and he winced. Even the slightest touch of anything against his face caused him pain. He brought his fingers to the wound and when he drew them away he saw a gob of blood on them and wished he never removed his bandages that morning.

Was he ever going to heal?

The two boys went inside the cabin while the girls remained on the deck. They were thin and pretty and held one another close. He thought for a moment they might kiss but all they did was hug. Consoling one another.

He could run and take them in an instant, snatching their life away before anyone knew what happened, but the man patiently held his ground. Better to wait for the cover of night, and then he would deal with these trespassers.

The wind kicked up and ruffled the dry leaves at his feet. He sniffed the air and looked at the sky. Even though it was bright blue and cloudless, a storm was coming. He could smell it. Off in the distance approaching like a thief to steal away the sun, making it dark forever.

The rain would soothe him.

He shifted his position and glanced at the minivan. It was muddy and old, much like him. They must have come in that, which meant they could leave in it at any time, but when? An hour? A day? Three? His good eye squinted at the vehicle as he thought.

One of the boys, the black one, came into view holding a bucket. He looked left, right, and ditched the dirty water inside it onto the ground. He was tall and muscular and when he stretched the man could see his calf muscles flex.

He wasn't like the white one who, like the girls, was thin and delicate.

He continued crouching. Breathing. His chest rising and falling.

Waiting.

His hand fell to his side and brushed the serrated hunting blade hanging from his belt.

FOUR

Hours later, when the cabin was cleaned to the best of their abilities and night had fallen over the woods, Trevor, Sarah, Amy, and Kincaid sat in the living room with beers in their hands and music on the stereo. A slight breeze blew through the room, rustling the curtains hanging open in front of the window that overlooked Whisper Lake. It didn't do much to blow out the stench, which still remained though not as strong. Neither of them thought it would ever go away, but it was faint enough to allow them all to rest with ease, but they all knew a few more coats of bleach would be in order tomorrow.

Trevor and Sarah had the couch, huddled close to one another, while Amy sat on the arm of a recliner Kincaid occupied, slowly sliding down into his lap.

She passed him the remainder of a joint and he gladly accepted it, taking a long haul and holding it in before Amy offered him her lips. He blew the smoke into her mouth and they kissed — hard.

"Oh, man," Kincaid choked, "that was just what the doctor ordered." He placed his arm around Amy's waist and held her closer.

Trevor and Sarah nodded in unison. Stoned and drunk. Their eyes glazed over like donuts.

It had been a heavy day, and everyone was still a little jumpy, but the substances helped calm their nerves.

Trevor sighed and reached for a bag of chips. Crumbs spilled out and onto his chest and he groaned.

Sarah leaned over and nibbled them one by one off of his shirt.

He cradled her head in his hand and shoved it lower, toward his groin. She resisted and slapped him on the leg.

"Not in front of everyone," she said.

Kincaid waived a hand at her. "Awe, come on. It's nothing I haven't seen before."

Amy gawked at him and he quickly recovered.

"I meant porn, baby. I swear."

She rolled her eyes and took a pull from her beer bottle. It went down smooth and she burped.

Trevor stared up at the ceiling and shook his head, feeling the warmth of his girlfriend next to him.

He still couldn't believe what they had gone through. Never in a million years did he ever think he would be in a position to have to clean up dead animals and blood. That was something reserved for slaughterhouse workers, not high school graduates.

He had vomited twice while doing the deed, and Kincaid had upchucked once. It took a while, but eventually they made the cabin presentable for occupying, and he had changed the bed sheets with a fresh set he had found up in his grandmother's closet.

Sarah still didn't know if they could sleep in there, but by God he was going to try.

Kincaid and Amy would take the couch, which was a pullout job with a thin, worn mattress in it. They opted out of sleeping in the second bedroom so they could all be closer to one another.

"You might hear a little squeaking tonight," he smiled, grabbing Amy's ass.

"Whatever," Sarah moaned. "I'm too tired to do anything."

Trevor snapped his head to the side and cocked an eyebrow at her.

"Really?"

"We can do it in the morning, baby. Just jack yourself off tonight, okay?"

Kincaid laughed at him and Amy tried to hold back a giggle by placing her hand over her mouth, but couldn't. The weed had gone to her head and her sounds came out in short, quick bursts through her fingers.

"Whatever," Trevor sighed.

A clap of thunder boomed outside and everyone jumped. Rain began falling onto the deck, making tiny clack-clack-clack noises that seeped in through the open windows.

"Just like that," Sarah said, amazed at how quickly the weather had turned.

"Just like that," Amy said, looking over her shoulder as the sky lit up from a flash of lightning.

"Perfect," Kincaid said.

Trevor glanced at him and frowned.

"I'm serious," he continued. "You couldn't have scripted this better."

"Scripted what, baby?"

"A horror movie. Four teens, trapped in the woods with a maniacal killer on the loose, and now it starts to thunder and lightning."

"There's no killer on the loose, idiot," Trevor said, chucking a cheese puff at him. "Come on, stop it. You'll scare the girls."

"I was already scared," said Sarah.

"Me too," Amy echoed.

"Well, stop it anyway."

Kincaid took a drink and smacked his lips together. "I'm just fuckin' with you, man. Still, you have to admit this is pretty cliché. You even got a black guy along for the ride."

"There was no black guy in Evil Dead," Trevor smiled.

Kincaid scoffed and kissed Amy on the breast.

A chill ran down her spine and she shivered, enjoying the feel of her lovers' lips on her. She leaned in over top of him and cradled his face in her hands, kissing him hard once again. She straddled his lap and he dropped his beer bottle on the ground. It landed with a thud and the remaining inch of liquid spilled out onto the hardwood.

"Hey, come on, man," Trevor groaned, "we just cleaned this place."

"Sorry, man. Duty calls."

"Forget about all that horror movie junk," Amy said, slowly rocking her hips back and forth.

"Whatever you say, baby."

"Do you really think it was a squatter?" Sarah asked, bending her leg under her on the couch and turning to face Trevor.

He shrugged. "Honestly? I don't know. That seems to be the most reasonable explanation, though. I mean, no one's come back here since we arrived."

"Maybe they saw us from the woods and took off."

"Probably."

She chewed away at the inside of her mouth, thinking.

Half of her wished they had never come to the cabin, but the other half—the stoned and drunk half—was enjoying herself and thought in the morning everything would be fine. Once the rain stopped and the sun warmed everything up, things would be a lot better and they could get to cleaning and afterward, some serious R and R. Trevor's parents had given him a week to get everything straightened out, but she suspected they'd be done long before that and could just enjoy themselves once all the heavy lifting was done.

She couldn't shake the feeling something wasn't right, though. When she closed her eyes she saw the dead deer staring back at her, and she knew she'd probably have nightmares about it and that frightened her. More than the thought there might be someone out there creeping on them. Sarah's dreams were always so much worse than reality, or so she always thought.

"Besides," Kincaid said, looking over Amy's shoulder, "if someone does come back, we'll be ready for them." He glanced over toward the kitchen.

Trevor knew what he meant. In one half of the double sink the sharp blades they had found were sitting in a mixture of bleach and water, the grime and blood slowly dissolving off of them.

He didn't think it would come to that, but it was a comforting thought nonetheless. He was never the fighting type, but he liked to assume if worse came to worse, he'd do what needed to be done to protect Sarah, and he knew Kincaid felt the same way.

His chest rose and fell slowly as another flash of lightning lit up the night sky. A rumbling boom of thunder followed it and the rain came harder and faster then.

"Come on," he said, slowly getting to his feet and tapping Sarah on the knee. "Let's go to bed."

She nodded, letting him take her hand to pull her up. She fell into him and he caught her, but just barely. They rocked together back and forth until the ground beneath their feet stopped wobbling.

"Seriously?" Kincaid asked, checking his watch. "It's only eleven o'clock."

"Dude, I'm beat," Trevor went over and held out his hand.

Kincaid slapped it and Trevor caught his fingers and locked eyes with his friend.

"Be safe tonight."

Kincaid nodded. "You too, brother."

"Ugh, too much machismo for me. Goodnight, Amy," Sarah waved a hand at her and stumbled into the bedroom.

"Night, babes," she called after her.

Trevor followed and shut the door behind him. It locked shut.

"It's just you and me now," Kincaid whispered, stroking Amy's hair back and around her ear.

She smiled at him and licked her lips, jumping off of his lap and getting on her knees in front of him.

She placed her hands on his legs and spread them, coming up slowly between the inverted V and reaching for the waistband of his shorts.

"Fuck me," he said.

"Soon," she purred.

She pulled them down and his dick sprang free. It was semi-hard and she peeled off her top before taking it in her hand and rubbing it against her tits.

"You ready?"

He closed his eyes and groaned when she went took him in her mouth, her head bobbing up and down.

"Best. Trip. Ever," he whispered.

From behind the closed bedroom door they heard a thud and Amy popped him out from between her lips and looked over her shoulder. Kincaid sat up; ready to pull his shorts back into place and charge through it, smashing the lock in the process.

Then they heard Sarah begin to moan and Amy laughed, stoking him slowly as he sat back in position on the recliner.

"I guess she wasn't that tired after all."

"Guess not."

Amy smiled and he placed his hand on the back of her head, guiding her mouth over him once more.

Outside the rain fell and the thunder rolled.

FIVE

He peered through the curtains at the boy and the girl on the bed. The cloth blew in the breeze covering and uncovering his eye, but he remained still. The rain soaked his face, dripping off his chin in hues of red and pink.

The boy was on top of her, thrusting away and defiling the place where he slept. The springs beneath them squeaked, and he clenched his fists together until his fingernails made tiny, half-moon divots in his skin.

He'd wait a little longer. Let them enjoy their last night together. Tomorrow he'd have to do something so he could once again get back to the place he called home, rather than have to hide out in the woods like an animal.

She would want it that way.

"Trevor," the girl whispered.

He sucked in a sharp breath of air and let it seep out from between clenched teeth while the boy leaned in and kissed his girl, his pale ass still rising and falling.

"Oh, baby," Trevor moaned.

Their rhythm quickened and the man blinked.

A flash of lightning illuminated the window, revealing his body to no one. They weren't paying attention.

He was big and thick and stood ramrod straight. Still and unmoving. His heavy boots left deep imprints in the soggy ground outside the window while the rain continued to fall all around him. When he decided it was time to step away, they would fill in with water and be washed away. Like he was never there.

Watching them.

His mind turned like clockwork, trying to understand how these kids could do the things they had done. Take over another man's dwelling without permission. Invade his home like it was their own. Sleep in someone else's bed.

Soiling it.

Throwing out the things he owned like they meant nothing to anyone.

He ground his teeth together and unclenched his fists. The blood rushed to the top of his skin, pumping hard to fill in the gaps left by his nails.

He kept watching.

SIX

The bright morning sun evaporated the previous night's rainfall and by noon it was impossible to tell the ground had been soaked just hours before.

Everyone woke around the same time, ten, and were already hard at work cleaning out the cabin after a quick breakfast of scrambled eggs and toast Trevor cooked up from the supply of goods they had brought.

Their hangover headaches had quickly subsided after putting food and coffee into their stomachs.

Amy was in the bathroom, scrubbing the toilet and floor, while Kincaid worked over the kitchen, emptying the sink of bleach and water and filling it again with hot suds to soak off the metal instruments they had found yesterday.

Trevor occupied the second bedroom, while Sarah was down on her hands and knees in the living room, a scrub brush tight in her hand working back and forth over the hardwood floors with a bucket of hot water beside her.

The cabin door was wide open, letting a soft warm breeze blow through the place, and their music was cranked high, echoing into the woods around them.

Outside, Whisper Lake rippled in the wind.

"The bedroom is not that bad," Trevor said, stepping out into the hallway with a garbage bag full of clothes in it. He dragged it across the floor and out onto the porch where it would sit until his father could come up with the trash removal company to dispose of everything.

"Hey, help me move the recliner," Sarah called. "I want to scrub under it."

Trevor walked with a spring in his step into the living room, feeling quite good about things now.

His night with Sarah had been perfect, and afterward they had fallen asleep naked in each other's arms. He awoke before her, stroking her soft, smooth shoulder until she stirred and looked up at him, her head resting comfortably on his chest.

Now her ass was on display before him and he looked down at her on her hands and knees, his groin stirring once again while he admired the shape of her in her cutoff shorts. He knew she wasn't wearing any underwear because he had watched her dress.

She looked back over her shoulder and winked up at him.

"Enjoying the view?"

He chuckled to himself and shuddered. "More than you know."

"Come on, give me a hand."

He dragged the recliner at one end as she pushed it from below. Dust kicked up from underneath it and she sneezed, waiving her hand in front of her face to clear it away.

"Look," Trevor said.

When her eyes stopped watering Sarah looked down at the ground.

Amy and Kincaid joined them in the living room when they heard Trevor's enthusiasm.

"What is it?" Sarah asked.

They were looking at a small trap door no bigger than a shoebox. It had a circular metal handle on one end but no lock. It crossed the grain of the hardwood floor, going perpendicular to the parallel wooden planks.

"Should I open it?" Sarah asked, looking up at Trevor and waiting for an answer.

"Sure, why not," he shrugged.

"Better not be no heads in there," Kincaid mumbled.

Amy nudged him with her shoulder and he swayed on his feet.

Sarah grabbed hold of the handle and hoisted the trap door. It yawned open all the way back until it was nearly level with the floor again.

She got to her feet, bracing her hand against Trevor's midsection for balance. He peered over the edge of the hole and into the darkness below.

"Looks to be at least a couple of feet deep," he mused.

He got down and reached his hand inside, feeling around to see if there was anything in it. He moved slowly, cautiously, not wanting anything to surprise him.

His fingers came upon something cold and hard and he flinched, yanking them back before grasping whatever it was and pulling it free.

"Holy shit," Kincaid's eyes went wide and his mouth turned down in a marveled grunt.

"Damn," Trevor said.

In his hand was an old, six-shooter revolver covered in a layer of dust and grime. He brought it eye-level and looked in the chambers.

"It's loaded."

He dusted it off, careful not to touch the trigger, and handed it to Kincaid. "Take a look."

"Ugh, I hate guns," Amy said.

Kincaid held it in both hands and aimed toward the kitchen, closing one eye and looking down the front sight.

Trevor reached back into the hole and pulled out a small box of bullets and placed them next to it. He reached in once again and brought out several small, leather bound books.

He flipped through them for a moment, his eyes scanning the pages.

"Looks like diary entries from my grandmother," he said.

Kincaid put the gun down on the coffee table and sat back in the recliner. "Babes, grab me a beer, would you?" he asked Amy.

"Anything else, your majesty?" she turned away annoyed and went to the fridge.

"Grab some for all of us," Trevor called after her. "I think it's about break time anyway."

He sat on the couch next to Sarah and put the journals on the coffee table, keeping one of them on his lap.

"Anyone up for story time?"

Amy returned with the beers and passed them around. "I am," she said, sitting on the floor next to Kincaid.

"Why not," Kincaid said, twisting off his cap.

Trevor took a healthy swig from his bottle and breathed deep.

He wasn't sure if he should be reading his grandmother's innermost thoughts to his friends, but they had all been through so much already it seemed only fair to not keep secrets from them. Besides, chances were whatever he read he was going to tell them about it anyway.

He cleared his throat and started.

"July 17th, 1992. He came to me again last night and we lied under the moon, our bodies coming together as one under the stars. I know I should feel guilty with Ben back at home but I just can't. Gunther treats me with respect and kindness, two things I am not used to. He makes me feel like I am twenty years old again and when he enters me it's like heaven raining down inside my body. He takes his time and pleasures me in ways I never thought possible. Who knew I could feel such sensations? I can't help but smile thinking about it again now. I only hope he returns tonight. Perhaps I can get to know him better? Find out where he's from and what he is doing out here all alone, with seemingly no place to go. I'm sure I'll learn more about him eventually, but for now I am quite enjoying the little mystery of our encounters."

Trevor closed the journal and looked at everyone.

Kincaid spoke first, saying, "Gunther? Dude, your grandmother was a freak!"

Amy elbowed him hard on the knee and his reflexes caused him to flinch. He rubbed the sore spot and glared at her.

"Unbelievable," Trevor whispered.

"Wow," Sarah proclaimed. "That's all I can say. Wow."

Trevor took another long pull off his beer and swallowed in two big gulps. He flipped open the journal again, shaking his head and scoffing at the thought of his grandma having an affair. He started reading once more.

"August 18th. Gunther and I spent the day together sitting out on the deck. We had a lunch of sandwiches I prepared, and washed them down with some wine I had tucked away in one of the cupboards. Afterward I lied in his arms telling him about my days in the theater, and he pleasured me with his hand, after which I found my head in his lap, pleasing him as he had pleased me. I feel like a schoolgirl writing this all down but it is the only place I can share these feelings, for I cannot keep them bottled up inside any longer. I want to scream to the world about Gunther and how he makes me feel, but I won't. Not to my daughters, and certainly not to my husband, who sits at home oblivious to my shenanigans here at the cabin he built for me, wasting his life away in that ratty old chair of his, watching TV and grunting at sports while he drinks himself into a stupor. Gunther is so unlike him, it's uncanny. Bigger, stronger—definitely stronger—yet soft at the same time. Gentle, like a summer breeze. If only it could be like this always, but I must return home soon and lead the double life I have now found myself in."

Trevor stopped and took another, longer, deep breath.

Sarah watched his face, looking for any signs he might be hurt by the discovery that his grandmother was an adulterer. He wasn't, though. He remained calm, his lip curling up into a grin as he closed the book and placed it back on the coffee table.

"Well," he said. "That's some grandma I had, huh?"

Amy laughed and buried her head in her knees. "Whoa," she said to the floor.

Kincaid finished his beer and placed the bottle down next to him, on the opposite side of her. He leaned forward in the recliner, resting his elbows on his legs and looking at his friend.

Trevor said nothing for a moment, but rather just sat back on the couch, taking it all in.

He didn't know how to feel, really, but he knew he didn't feel bad. His mother had once told him his grandfather was a taskmaster of sorts, always barking orders and whatnot to her mother. It stemmed from his Army days, she said. If that were the case, then how could he blame his grandmother for falling into the arms of another man? He'd do it if he were placed in the same situation. A loveless marriage, with only a few days out of the year to get away from it. She had to cut loose or else risk going crazy.

He ran his hands down the side of his face, sighing and pulling the skin beneath his eyes with him. He looked at Sarah and she turned away, disgusted by his appearance.

"Sorry," he said.

She patted him on the knee. "Boys will be boys."

"So what now?" Kincaid finally asked.

Trevor got up and stretched, reaching toward the ceiling. His shirt pulled up, exposing his stomach. Sarah reached out and tickled him, causing Trevor to double over in surprise and start chuckling.

He's going to be okay, she thought.

"Now, we get back to work. At least for another hour and then we'll stop and grab some food."

"Sounds good to me," Kincaid said. He got up from his seat and picked up the revolver. "Hey, at least now we got some protection." He flashed a wide grin, exposing his teeth to Amy.

"Whatever," she shook her head and walked past him and back into the bathroom.

Trevor gave him an inquisitive look but Kincaid waived him off. *Who knows what her problem is*, it said.

Sarah kissed him on the lips and closed the trap door, getting back down on her hands and knees to scrub the area under the recliner.

Trevor took one last look at her ass and went back into the second bedroom, leaving the small leather journals on the coffee table.

SEVEN

The rest of the day passed without incident. The kids worked hard to get the cabin in tip top shape for resale; scrubbing, waxing, cleaning, and polishing as much as they could until their muscles were sore and their feet ached.

Come diner time they all sat around in the living room, ignoring grandma's journals and opting to concentrate on their food, which consisted of toasted sandwiches with lunchmeat on them, chips, and soda pop. The beer would come later. As would more weed.

A delightful reward after a hard day's work.

Since their break earlier, Trevor noticed Amy and Kincaid still weren't getting along, and he tried to pull him aside to find out why, but Kincaid was having none of it. He was frustrated beyond belief, so Trevor commented to Sarah and she said she noticed it too.

When she tried to talk to Amy, she got the same reaction.

It boiled over to the point where they were sitting in awkward silence, eating quietly while the stereo played in the background.

The sun hung low in the sky, preparing to sleep for the evening, and it cast a soft orange glow over the water.

"Pretty," Sarah commented, taking a bite of her sandwich.

Trevor nodded and crunched a chip, glancing at Kincaid who seemed to think his food was the most interesting thing on the planet because it was all he kept staring at.

Trevor glanced at Sarah and she shook her head, knowing he was thinking about saying something. He rolled his eyes and kept eating.

"So," Sarah chirped when they were finished, "who's up for a game of Monopoly?"

Amy shook her head, as did Kincaid. "Not me," he said.

"Not me," Amy mimicked in a low-pitched voice.

Kincaid threw his paper plate to the floor and bounced to his feet.

"That's it, I'm outta here."

"What? Where are you going?"

"Crazy!" He stormed down the hall, past the kitchen, and to the front door which was now closed. He threw it open, bubbling over with rage.

Amy turned away from her friends, feeling embarrassed not only for herself, but also for her boyfriend. He was making a complete ass out of himself when they should have all been having a good time.

"Fuck me!" Kincaid yelled. "You better get out here Trevor and clean this shit up, I'm done."

Trevor stood and watched him blow out of the cabin. There was something on the ground in front of the door, hiding in shadow.

He strode to the front of the cabin and recoiled in horror when he came upon the threshold leading outside.

"Oh God," he gasped.

Sarah quickly rushed to his side but Amy stayed behind, sulking. Not even the slightest bit interested in what they were seeing.

Trevor stumbled back and Sarah ran into him, glancing over his shoulder at the ground outside the door.

She yelped in shock.

There was a dead fox on the ground in front of the cabin, just outside the door. It was gutted, with its insides on the outside, and its tongue pulled out through a slit in its throat. Its dirty red fur quivered in the wind.

"Kincaid," Trevor called after his friend. "Kincaid!"

The sound of her boyfriend's name caused Amy to stir and she got to her feet, slowly walking toward the kitchen. Sarah heard her coming and turned to face her.

"Amy, don't," she said.

All that did was fill her with a sense of dread something awful had happened.

She brushed past Sarah and looked at the dead animal on the stoop.

"Jesus!" Tears formed at the corner of her eyes as she felt her emotions getting the better of her. She cried out and ran forward, looking to make a quick exit, but Trevor grabbed her around the waist and held her back.

"Sarah, help me!"

She slammed the door shut and locked it while Amy threw a fit in Trevor's arms.

"No, let me go! He's out there. We have to go find him."

"He'll be okay," Trevor grimaced. Amy was a fighter. Kicking and screaming, squirming under his arms. She probably would have gotten away if she had bit him, but instead he dragged her back into the living room and threw her to the couch.

"Be careful," Sarah yelled.

He ran his hands through his hair. His heart was racing and his face had turned beet red with anger and frustration.

What the hell was Kincaid thinking going out in the woods after seeing that shit?

Amy sobbed into Sarah's arms and Trevor watched as she held her tight, rocking her back and forth slowly, letting her cry into her chest.

"Shhh," she consoled, rubbing Amy's back. "It'll be okay."

"Kincaid's a big boy," Trevor said, trying to help. "He can take care of himself. We just need to stay calm and wait for him to get back. Let him blow off some steam."

He grabbed for the revolver and held it tight in his hands.

"What are you going to do with that?" Sarah asked.

He shook his head, too freaked out to say anything else. All he could think about was Kincaid out in those woods all alone, without anything to keep him safe. He couldn't leave the girls all by themselves, though. He was stuck.

"Dammit," he cursed under his breath, looking back toward the front door.

Kincaid was already far away from it, striding deeper and deeper into the woods. He huffed through the brush, tearing through thin tree branches and pulling them loose, using them as switches to bat away stray foliage.

The nerve of Amy mimicking him like that. All day she had been on his ass when all he wanted was to be left alone. After what happened the night before he felt so fucking stupid and petty. Even though she had told him it was okay, he couldn't help but think it wasn't.

It was the first time anything like that had happened to him, and it made him feel about two feet tall.

They had been there having a good time, he in the chair and her down on the floor in front of him on her knees. She pleased him for a while until it was time to pull out the sofa, which they did together. Only when they got naked and under the sheets, he couldn't perform. In the time it took to get the bed ready, his dick had gone softer than melted cheese and no matter what she tried to do; he just couldn't get hard again.

He went down on her when she asked but his heart wasn't in it. He was too frustrated with his body and sour at Amy for still making him please her when all he wanted to do was roll over to stir in his own misery and fall asleep.

"It's okay, baby. Don't worry about it. These things happen."

"Not to me, they don't."

They eventually fell asleep but when he woke up he was still sore about the whole experience and got even grouchier when he saw how happy Trevor and Sarah were. It made him feel inferior. Like less of a man.

Amy was pissy with him too, but he had no idea it was because of the way he was acting. He thought all her talk about it being okay was just for show, and she really was mad at him for not being able to get it up.

Now he swore and screamed to the woods, frustrated he left his friends behind. That had been a fox on the ground in front of the cabin and he glimpsed at how badly mangled it was and in that second knew he should just stay, but he had already made a spectacle of himself and couldn't take it back. He had to keep going for his own sake, or else risk seeing the looks on everyone's faces when he chickened out because of some stupid dead animal. He couldn't take that.

Not now.

He kicked what he thought was a branch but turned out to be a root embedded in the ground and stubbed his toe. He toppled over, falling hard to the ground and staring up at the sky. The first remnants of stars were beginning to appear as the sun went down, cloaking him in darkness.

"Shit," he mumbled.

Something, or someone, had done that to the fox. The way it was torn apart like that, he opted to think it was a person rather than another animal, and a chill went up and down his spine at the thought of whoever it was still out there in the woods.

With him.

Suddenly every little noise became cause for concern. A snake slithering through dry leaves, an owl hooting high overhead. A bird cawing off in the distance. He jumped at it all, eager to get back to the cabin now that he was truly afraid.

Only he didn't know where the cabin was.

He turned and faced in every direction, but the fall had disoriented his position and Kincaid couldn't tell where he was. He had gone too far into the woods and now he was lost.

"Fuck me. This is fucking perfect," he yelled, feeling the first hot sting of tears form in his eyes.

A louder, more pronounced noise off to his right gave him cause for concern. It sounded like an actual branch breaking off a tree. He didn't know of any bird that could do that.

"Hello?" he called out. "Trev?"

He half expected his friend to come running into him just to get him back for tearing away from them like that, but no one was there.

Kincaid stopped and listened for the thud of feet pounding against the woodland floor, but heard nothing.

Panic stricken, he started to run, but had no idea he was actually going deeper and deeper into the woods with each step. When it was clear he was getting nowhere, he turned and ran in the opposite direction, swerving left, then right, hoping to come across some landmark that would tell him he was going the correct way. Back toward the cabin he never should have left in the first place.

Kincaid stopped to catch his breath and fell to his knees. Anger and dread filled him and he started crying, clutching his face in his hands and wailing into the night for someone to come and save him.

He sobbed so loud and hard he never heard the man come up behind him, towering over his frame and watching him from behind through one good eye.

The only thing he felt was the tug on his hair as his head was pulled back, but he had no time to react as the serrated blade was dragged across his throat so quickly he felt no pain until the blood started spilling out over his chest.

His hands came up and wrapped themselves around the wound, trying to stop the flow of life, and the man came out from behind him and stood in front of Kincaid, hovering above him. His chest rising and falling steadily.

Kincaid tried to speak but couldn't. His voice just came in raspy bursts that gurgled with blood.

He had no problem screaming though, when the man clutched his forehead, tilted his head back, and kept cutting.

EIGHT

Amy had calmed down enough to the point where she at least stopped sobbing and Sarah could let go of her. She handed her friend a tissue and encouraged her to blow her nose.

"You look like shit," Sarah said.

Amy looked at her with puffy red eyes and scowled.

Trevor continued to pace back and forth, trying to figure out what he could do.

Leaving the girls alone was not an option, but it had been nearly an hour since Kincaid had taken off, and there was no sign of him returning any time soon. He poked his head out the kitchen window, peeling back the curtains, and there was no movement from outside except the trees.

But night had fallen now and it was hard to see. Clouds covered the sky, threatening rain again. Blocking out the full moon.

Sarah came up behind him and wrapped her arms around his waist, forcing him to stand still for a moment.

"You think he's okay?" she whispered, not wanting to alarm Amy.

Trevor shook his head. "I don't know."

He glanced over and kissed her on the forehead. Amy wasn't the only one he didn't want to alarm.

"I think he'll be fine, but I can't get that fox out of my head. I mean, it's right outside still."

Sarah agreed with him and released Trevor from her grasp. He spun around and placed the revolver on the kitchen counter, embracing her fully.

"Well I'm glad you two can be okay with this," Amy shouted from the living room.

Trevor let go of Sarah, grabbed the gun, and walked back to where she was sitting, taking a seat across from her in the recliner.

"Amy, it's not that we don't care. We do. We just don't know what we're dealing with here."

"That's all the more reason to take the gun and go out there and find him."

He knew she was right, and he wanted nothing more than to go find Kincaid and make sure he was okay, but in all honesty Trevor was afraid. Yeah, he was sure the guy would be fine, but what if he wasn't? What if someone was out there fucking with them all and was just waiting for the right moment to strike? The moment he opened the front door?

"We can't do that, Amy."

"Why not?"

"Because what if Trevor goes out there, leaving us all alone, and something else happens and he's not here," Sarah said.

Trevor glanced at her, his facial features softening, thanking her for taking his side.

Amy didn't have an answer for her. She threw her hands up into the air and slammed her body back against the couch cushions, frustrated to all hell.

Trevor reached for one of his grandmother's journals and flipped through it.

"What are you thinking?" Sarah asked him, leaning forward. Hopeful.

"I don't know. Maybe there's something in here that mentions squatters or someone else hanging around in the woods."

"There is someone hanging around in the woods," Amy said quietly.

They looked at her but said nothing. Waiting.

"Gunther," she said,

"Amy, that was twenty years ago. For all we know he's dead and buried."

"Yeah," Sarah added. "Or long gone."

Trevor stopped turning the pages and sat back to read.

"July 29th. No year. I fear that Gunther may not make it through the night, even with my training as a nurse. My supplies here are limited and I just don't know if I have everything I need to bring him through his injuries."

"Wait," Sarah interrupted. "What injuries? Go back a few entries."

Trevor, sensing the journals might hold the key to what was happening, eagerly began searching for an entry his grandmother made that might tell them more about the mysterious Gunther.

"Here. July 27th. Same, no year. My God, what a horrible day it has been. Gunther is now seriously injured and I just don't know what I can do to help him. There was a terrible grease fire and he has been burned beyond recognition. His face seemed to go up in flames and melt off. His hair has been burned, as well as his neck and chest. He has most certainly lost sight in his left eye, and one of his nostrils has been closed off. My training as a nurse is limited and what few supplies I have up at the cabin surely cannot be enough to sustain him, though I will do my best. He is resting now in the bed, as I have bandaged him up as best I can for the time being. He wails and moans in his sleep, crying out, and I have to change the dressing every couple of hours so he does not get further infected.

"He was in the process of fixing my car when it happened but never finished. He stopped to make us something to eat when the terrible fire happened. I managed to squelch it with baking soda and the small extinguisher I keep on hand for emergencies, but the damage was already done by the time I got to Gunther. I have no idea how automotives work, so I cannot finish his repairs myself and take him to a hospital. All I can do is pray and wait and hope he survives, though I suspect if he does he will never be the same again."

Trevor closed the journal, and his eyes, imagining a deranged madman in the woods stalking Kincaid.

"Jesus," Sarah mumbled. "That's awful. Imagine having to go through something like that. Do you think he survived?"

"Obviously," Amy added.

Sarah shook her head, amazed at her pessimism.

Trevor opened his eyes and picked up another journal.

"Let's find out," he said.

Sarah reached out and took Amy's hand, making a small amends and trying to make them both feel better through some good old human contact. Amy gave it a faint squeeze and half-smiled, grateful to have her friend with her.

"June 18th, of what I can only assume is the following year? I don't know; she stopped writing the years down. Gunther is doing much better now, though he has developed somewhat of a temper since his ordeal last summer. He thinks I don't love him anymore because of the way he looks, but I have assured him that I do, and have even tried to copulate with him on several occasions to prove it, but to no avail. He hates the world these days and all he wants to do is stay inside instead of going out and enjoying the sun like we used to do, even though there is no one around to see him."

"Well, there's your answer," Amy said, releasing Sarah's hand and choking back a sob. "Kincaid is out there, with that man, and who knows what he's doing to him."

Trevor threw the journal on the coffee table with the others. They toppled over and spread out over one another. There were seven in all.

"Jesus Christ, Amy," he snapped. There was no way Gunther was still alive, and even if he were he'd be an old man by now. At least seventy, seventy-five perhaps? Frail and fragile and in no shape to do anything to anyone. Not with those injuries and frame of mind. He'd probably gone crazy and offed himself. Maybe even in front of Trevor's grandmother.

Who knows?

He'd have to keep reading her journals to find out for sure, but he was spent. Too tired to even think straight. He just wanted Kincaid to come back safe and sound, and from there they could figure out a course of action.

The cabin was good enough, he decided. His parents would have to deal with the rest of it. Surely they would understand if he came home early if he just explained what to them what happened. Bring grandma's journals with him. His mother would be hurt to read them, no doubt. Discovering your own mother had an affair with some backwoods stranger would be quite a shock to the system. She'd get over it though, if it meant he was safe and back home with them once she understood just what exactly they had been through.

There was a loud, sickening thud at the front door and Amy jumped to her feet.

"Kincaid!"

Trevor tried to reach out and grab her but he was too late. His fingers brushed the fabric of her shirt and even Sarah, who was sprier and quicker than he was, missed out on catching her.

"Amy!" she called. "Wait!"

"It might not be him," Trevor shouted.

He sighed and shook his head at Sarah, and together they ran after Amy, hoping like hell it *was* Kincaid at the door, trying to get in after a lengthy walk in the woods to cool off only to find it locked.

Amy reached it first, steadied herself, took a deep breath and gripped the handle for a moment before unlocking it and throwing it open.

Trevor and Sarah joined her just as it finished creaking on its hinges, and looked over her shoulders.

There was no one at the door.

Amy's heart sank and she felt the tears welling up in her eyes yet again. It was hopeless. He wasn't coming back. Her head hung low and she blinked, looking at the mangled fox at her feet, only...there was something else there.

It was—

She shrieked, causing goosebumps to rise on Sarah and Trevor's skin, and the hair to prick up on the back of their necks. Never in their entire life had they heard such a sound come from one human being. It was ghoulish.

Amy stumbled backward, pointing past the torn apart fox, covering her mouth with one hand. She trembled to her very core and fell over.

Trevor and Sarah were hopeless to help her.

They were too busy gazing upon the severed head of Kincaid.

NINE

Trevor, in a last ditch effort to keep control of his own sanity, ran back into the cabin and grabbed the keys to the minivan as well as his grandmother's revolver, though he forgot to snatch up the box of bullets they had found with it.

He rushed to the front door, hoisted Amy to her feet and grabbed Sarah's arm.

"Come on," he screamed. "We're getting the fuck out of here right now."

He stepped delicately over the fox, and Kincaid's lifeless head.

The eyes were still open and they stared up at him, and Trevor thought for a brief moment it was a lie. That wasn't Kincaid's head. It belonged to a life-like doll. Someone was playing a trick on them, and in a minute Kincaid would jump out and they'd all have a good laugh over it once things calmed down.

Blood dripped from the torn neck flesh and onto the porch in slow, methodical drops, and Trevor blinked. Somehow that made it all the more real and he felt the bile rise in his throat but he couldn't lose it. Not now. The girls needed him to be strong because if he wasn't, than who would be? Sarah? Amy? Certainly not Amy. She was almost lost to them now. Pushed too far. Over the edge and tumbling downward into craziness. He could see it in her frightened, swollen eyes.

Sarah helped him get her out of the cabin, making sure to avert her eyes from Kincaid's head as much as she could. Amy tried to look down but Sarah slapped her. Told her to look at the minivan instead.

Their escape.

"Come on," Trevor urged once they were past the porch.

The keys jingled in his hand as he fumbled to find the one that opened the door. Then he remembered it was unlocked, and he paused.

"Wait," he said, stopping Amy and Sarah from going any further.

He approached the vehicle with the revolver raised, ready to fire at anything that moved. It was too dark to see inside it so he quickly opened the driver's side door so at least the dome light would come on.

Nothing in the front seat. Nothing in the back seat.

Nothing in the trunk.

The coast was clear. No one would be able to rise up and slice them to pieces from behind.

He waived the girls forward and hurried them into their seats. Sarah crawled into the passenger side from his open door, and Amy jumped in back when he slid the side door open. He slammed it shut and she whimpered at the sound. Noise — any noise — was just too much for her to handle.

Trevor hopped in and shut his door, immediately engaging the power locks. They clicked shut, trapping them inside the minivan.

"Hurry, hurry!" Sarah said. Her voice was shaking, just like the rest of her.

Trevor found the right key and slid it into the ignition.

"Here we —"

He turned it.

Nothing happened.

The color drained from his face and he tried again.

And again.

And again.

Nothing.

"What? What's the matter?" Sarah cried.

"Wait here."

He jumped out of the vehicle and disengaged the hood before slamming the door shut. Sarah continued screaming at him, but her shouts were muffled once he was on the outside looking in. He glanced at her through the windshield before throwing the hood open and checking the engine. She was already shaking her head.

Destroyed.

The entire engine was a wreck. Someone had ripped out all the wires with their bare hands and proceeded to stab it repeatedly until fluid and oil seeped out of every orifice.

"Fuck me!"

He thought he heard something over his shoulder and turned quickly to look, raising his hand to fire the gun, but his hand was empty. He had left the revolver on the seat.

He rushed to his side of the vehicle, threw open the door once more and grabbed for it. When he turned back around to face the open woods, nothing moved but the trees in the soft breeze of night.

Sweat poured off of him and down the side of his face and Trevor wiped as much of it away as he could. His eardrums thumped in unison with the beating of his heart and he swallowed — hard — trying to find his voice.

This isn't happening, he told himself. All he wanted to do was clean out the damn cabin. Was that so hard to ask? Why was Gunther (no, not Gunther. Gunther was dead) doing this to them?

His knees felt weak and he thought he might collapse so he braced himself on the driver's side mirror. He heard a thud and moments later Sarah came around front to steady him. She cradled his face in her trembling hands and forced him to look her in the eyes.

"Stay with me, baby. Stay with me. We gotta go."

His eyes were vacant. Like he was somewhere else in his head. Lost to her.

Sarah reeled her arm back and slapped him hard across the face.

He blinked and brought his fingers to the red mark on his cheek. He shook his head rapidly from side to side and squeezed his eyes shut, grinding his jaw back and forth.

"Son of a bitch," he said.

"There you are," Sarah said. "Come on, let's go."

He looked at the minivan and at Amy in the back seat. She was rocking slowly back and forth, not paying attention to anything or anyone.

"Go where?"

"Back to the cabin."

The cabin. Of course. It was the only other place they could find sanctuary. His grandmother knew it, and so did he.

Trevor cracked his neck and rushed to the side of the minivan. He got the door open and hauled Amy out.

She didn't protest.

Sarah took up the other side of her and together they stumbled back toward the front door where the fox and Kincaid's severed head lie. She hoped like hell Amy was too far gone to even notice. They'd work on bringing her back once they were safe and secure inside the four walls of the cabin, where nothing could get to them.

They all managed without staring too long at what was left of Kincaid, though for a moment Trevor wondered if he should bring the head inside. It didn't seem right, leaving him there like that.

He shook off the feeling and slammed the cabin door shut.

That was nuts.

He bolted the lock and ushered everyone back to the living room. Sarah sat Amy down on the couch while he went and shut all the windows, locking them in place. He then went from room to room once more, inspecting them to make sure no one had snuck in while they had been hopelessly trying to make a run for it in the minivan.

The cabin was empty.

Satisfied, he went to the kitchen, picked up a handful of knives, and brought them back to the girls, scattering them on the floor at their feet.

"Just in case," he eyeballed Sarah and she nodded.

He sat back in the recliner, trying to catch his breath so he could think of something, anything, they could do to survive.

"So that's it?" Amy whispered.

Trevor and Sarah looked at her, amazed she was able to say anything at all.

She brought her eyes up to meet theirs and stared intently at her two friends.

"We're dead, aren't we?" she asked.

She was there, but she wasn't. She looked to be a shell of her former self. Of the Amy they all knew and loved. She was there in body only, but they could see the writing on the wall; she would never be the same again.

None of them would.

"No," Sarah said. "Not yet."

Then the lights went out, and they all screamed.

TEN

"What the fuck?' Sarah grabbed hold of Amy for safety but it was like taking hold of a sack of flour. Heavy and lifeless.

"He's cut the power," Trevor said.

Their eyes adjusted to the darkness and at that moment the clouds parted to let at least some of the full moon shine in through the front window overlooking Whisper Lake.

"Come on, help me find some candles," he said, getting to his feet and glancing in Sarah's general direction.

"Wait here," she said to Amy, "I'll be right back."

"We're dead, we're dead, we're dead, we're dead," her friend mumbled over and over.

It sent a chill down Sarah's spine and she thought about slapping her again, but knew it would be useless. The only person who could save Amy now, was Amy.

She and Trevor stumbled around the cabin in the dark looking for candles. They found several of the scented ones they had brought with them, and proceeded to light them one by one, disbursing them to the various rooms, with four in the living room because that's where they needed the most light.

"This is bad," she whispered to him when they took two back to the second bedroom.

Trevor's bottom lip quivered and she held him tight, thankful he was acting like a person and not some macho asshole who was trying to play the hero and would do nothing more than get them all killed.

"I just keep seeing Kincaid," she said through sporadic tears.

"Me too."

He breathed in her scent, sweat mixed with the antiperspirant she used that smelled like lilacs. Slowly he calmed himself. Having her close to him helped him hold on to something worth fighting for because Lord knew if it were just he and Amy, he would have probably given up a long time ago.

"What are we going to do?"

Trevor rubbed her back for a moment before pulling away, holding Sarah at arm's length and looking her in the eyes.

"We're going to live."

She steeled her trembling lip and nodded.

Sarah never loved him more than in that second.

"Come on," he kissed her on the lips and they went back to the living room to sit with Amy and make sure she way okay while at the same time trying to come up with a plan to get the hell out of there.

Every shadow that passed in front of the windows startled Trevor, but none of them belonged to Gunther, who he had now accepted was the only person who could be doing this to them because it was the only thing that made sense, and he had to make sense of it all to keep himself grounded.

Try as he might to deny it, Amy was right. Gunther was alive.

His eyes scanned the pile of journals still sitting on the coffee table and he reached for one.

"Seriously?" Sarah frowned.

"I don't know what else to do, Sar. My grandmother obviously knew a lot about this guy, so maybe there's something in here that can help us."

He ignored her disapproving gestures and flipped through the pages, searching for words, sentences, anything that might give them a clue as to why Gunther was doing this.

"June 9th. I returned home today after a long walk to clear my head, only to find the cabin in disarray. I fear Gunther has gone over the edge now, past the brink of sanity. His speech is impaired; his facial features are twisted and deformed like a wax sculpture left out in the sun too long, and his mind is not what it used to be. I just don't know what to do with him anymore, but I do know I cannot continue down this path much longer. What used to bring such joy and happiness to my heart only brings pain and suffering now. I may as well just stay home with Ben if it's going to be like this, for Gunther is no longer than man I first met. He's slowly becoming a monster and I fear for my safety when he gets in these fits of his. No reasoning helps, nor do my tears. He ignores it all in favor of his own madness until he tires himself out and collapses in a heap on the floor. Most times I just leave him there now, when before I would at least try and pry him to the bed or couch. He's too heavy for me, though. My strength is not what it used to be, though his seems to be increasing tenfold the older he gets."

Trevor stopped reading as the wind kicked up outside, blowing dry summer leaves across the deck in front of the window next to him.

He closed the journal and sighed, tossing it back on the table with the others.

"So, what?" Sarah asked. "We're just supposed to wait until this all blows over and Gunther tires himself out?"

"I don't know."

Amy twitched next to her and Sarah clenched her jaw open and shut. She was getting tired and frustrated with having to babysit the girl like she was some invalid who couldn't take of herself. Yeah, her boyfriend had just been murdered and that was hard to deal with, but for crying out loud they were all fighting for their lives now. Amy included. How could she just lie down and give up like this?

"Without the van there's not much we can do," Trevor continued. "There's no place to go. All we have is this gun that we don't even know works, and some sharp knives. Is that enough to stop him if he comes bursting through the door? From the way my grandmother makes it sound, he's an unstoppable psycho now. I just don't know if it'll be enough."

"I wish Kincaid were here," Sarah said.

Amy sucked in a sharp breath of air at the sound of his name.

"Shut up," she added.

"Sarah!" Trevor scolded.

"What?" she got to her feet and began pacing back and forth. "I'm sorry," she yelled. "I'm tired and angry and I just can't take her anymore. Excuse me for wanting to live."

Trevor threw his hands into the air as if giving up.

Amy sat across from him. A vegetable. He felt his girlfriend's frustration every time he looked at her. She was doing nothing to help herself, nor was she contributing anything to the conversation. She was a goner if he ever saw one. Still, Sarah didn't need to lash out at her like that. It was hard on all of them. This was just her way of dealing with it, whether they liked it or now.

"I just wish we had *something*," Sarah said.

"Tell me about it. What I wouldn't give for a fucking Internet connection right now or a cell—"

"Cellphone!" Sarah screamed. "My cellphone."

She ran into their bedroom and Trevor quickly followed.

"Sarah," he groaned. "There's no signal up here, remember?"

"Well I have to fucking try," she said, rummaging through her suitcase. "It's more than I can say for that thing out there," she motioned back toward the living room.

She got her phone free and powered it up.

"Come on, come on," she mumbled to herself, hopping up and down on the balls of her feet like she needed to pee.

Trevor leaned against the doorframe and folded his arms across his chest, watching her fruitless efforts with a sense of sadness in his heart. She was going to be so disappointed when she found out her phone didn't work.

"I have a bar!" she proclaimed.

"What?" his eyes widened and he went to her side, looking over her shoulder at the screen.

"Oh, now it's gone. Step back."

Trevor did, and with a flicker of hope in his mind that sent a shot of adrenaline coursing through his veins. Where there was one bar, there might be another.

"Still gone."

She began wandering around the cabin, holding her phone out and looking for a signal. A bar would appear intermittently, but disappear before she could get a lock on it. It was something, though.

"It's these damn walls," she said, looking all around them at the enclosed space. "I bet if I could get outside I could at least dial 911 or something."

"Well we can't do that," Trevor said. "Absolutely not."

"So, what? We're just going to stay in here knowing there's at least a chance we can be saved if we just tried a little harder?"

"Sarah, I can't let you go out there, you know that. Gunther might be—"

"Oh, fuck Gunther," she screamed. She turned around and around in circle, screaming at the top of her lungs. "FUCK GUNTHER! YOU HEAR ME! FUCK YOU!"

"Stop it!" Amy put her hands over her ears and Sarah stopped moving.

Her bosom rose and fell like ocean waves and her body glistened with sweat.

The only sound anyone could hear was her breathing. Quick and shallow.

She was losing it.

Trevor went to her side and placed a comforting hand on her bare shoulder. He reached for the cellphone but she yanked her hand away and pulled loose from his grasp.

"I have to try," she pleaded. "Please let me try."

"Where would you go?"

She shook her head and looked up for an answer, hoping one would just fall from the sky, crash through the cabin roof and land in her lap.

The roof.

"The roof," she whispered.

"What?" Trevor leaned in to hear her better.

"The roof," she said louder.

He looked up along with her, his neck lifting so his eyes could see what she was seeing. He didn't get it.

"The roof?" he repeated.

"Yeah. I could climb up there to get a signal. Gunther can't reach me up there, right?"

"I...I don't know," Trevor admitted. "I never thought about it."

It seemed plausible, he guessed, but they wouldn't know for sure unless they tried, and suddenly he found himself adopting her never-give-up attitude.

He looked on her with wondrous fascination, admiring her strength and courage, but at the same time wanting to do everything in his power to protect her.

Her neck outstretched, her chest rising and falling, her muscles flexing in the candlelight. She was beautiful, and he would do anything for her.

"I'll go," he finally said.

She kept staring at the ceiling, as if his words didn't register with her. She licked her bottom lip and began shaking her head, the wheels in her mind continuously turning over and over.

"No. No, it has to be me."

"What? Why?"

She looked at him then and smiled. "Because you have to stay here and protect Amy."

Trevor glanced over his shoulder at the girl on the sofa.

Amy stared at him, this time with a look of hope in her eyes that she could be saved. She had been listening to them talk, and when Trevor caught her eye, her mouth fell open as if to say something, but no words came out.

He snapped his gaze back to Sarah, and asked, "How are you going to get up there?"

"I'll climb out the bedroom window," she immediately said, as if she had been thinking about it the entire time. "It's only about five feet to the roof from there. I can stand on the sill and pull myself up. You can spot me from the inside."

"Spot you?"

"Seven years of gymnastics, baby. I can do this in my sleep. I just need someone to help me keep my balance, and look out for...you know."

"Yeah," he whispered. "I know."

They both stood next to one another. Unmoving. Their shoulders brushing together.

For Trevor it wasn't a question of could this work, more a question of would this work? He had every faith Sarah could get to the roof with no problems, but he was more worried about the madman outside the cabin and what he would try and do. Would Trevor be able to haul her back inside in time and close the window if something were to happen? He didn't feel the same confidence she felt and it bugged him.

"You can do it," Amy whispered from the couch.

Sarah and Trevor looked at her and it was as if that's all they needed to hear to get moving. If the crazy girl sitting on her ass believed in them, then yes. They could do it.

Sarah went over and wrapped her arms tight around Amy, and for the first time in a while her friend reciprocated the gesture, as if finally understanding the gravity of the situation and what they were about to attempt.

"I love you," Sarah said.

Tears spilled out from her eyes and she felt Amy shake and sob against her.

"I love you, too."

They pulled away from one another and Sarah brushed Amy's hair out of her eyes.

"We're going to be okay," she said.

Amy nodded. "I know."

Sarah stood and took Trevor into the bedroom with her. She placed the cellphone in the pocket of her cutoffs and stared at him.

"This is nuts," he said.

"I know."

"Fuck, I love you," he held her close. Closer than he had ever held her before. In his mind, in his heart, against his body. She was one with him and he with her. He was going to marry that girl one day, of that he was certain.

"I love you so much, baby," she whispered into his chest.

"We can do this, we can do this, we can do this," he said over and over, stroking her hair.

She nodded her chin against him before pulling away.

They kissed a long, hard, passionate kiss. The kind of kiss you see in the movies between two people who were meant to be together but were separated through fate, only to find one another again before the end credits roll.

It was electric.

"You ready?" she asked.

Trevor nodded. "Yeah."

"Let's go."

She watched while he opened the bedroom window, letting a warm breeze blow through her hair.

ELEVEN

Trevor slowly stuck his head out and looked left, and then right.

No Gunther.

He waived Sarah forward and helped her up, hoisting her through the window so her legs and feet were facing him on the inside, while her upper body was outside, and her ass was resting comfortably on the sill.

She took a deep breath before carefully and methodically beginning to stand. She looked up at the edge of the roof taunting her, keeping her eyes focused on the prize. She placed one foot on the sill, and then the other, bracing herself against the outside of the cabin. Leverage would be difficult to find but if she could jump at just the right moment, she could catch the edge of the roof and pull herself up.

It would have to work.

"You good?" Trevor whispered.

She looked down at his head peeking out beside her legs and couldn't help but smile.

"Best view you've had in a while, huh?"

He grinned and gave her a thumbs up, feeling more confident now than ever that this crazy plan of theirs might pull them through.

"I need you to hold your hand out," she said. "I'm going to use it as a jumping off point."

Trevor nodded and stuck his arm out the window, holding his flat palm out and up as high as it would go. Sarah stuck a foot on it but he faltered.

"Hold on," Trevor said.

He joined his free arm with it for support and put one palm in the other. "Better?"

She tried again and this time the support was more secure.

"Better."

Droplets of rain began sprinkling her face and she knew she had to hurry or else the roof would be too slick to grasp. She'd worry about how the hell she was going to get down later.

With a deep breath she steeled her nerves as best she could and braced one foot on Trevor's outstretched palms. She glanced down at him, blew him a kiss, and said, "Here goes nothing."

Then she jumped as high as she could.

Sarah's fingers gripped the edge of the roof and held tight to it. She lost some of her balance though, and had trouble pulling herself up until Trevor unexpectedly hoisted himself out the window halfway and shoved her feet from below, allowing her to adjust herself and gather the strength needed to pull up.

She swung one foot over the edge, and then the other.

She did it.

Sarah was on the roof.

She gasped in exhaustion and looked over the edge at Trevor, who was still sitting on the sill. She smiled and blew him another kiss and then noticed something move out of the corner of her eye. She looked to the right and saw a massive figure lumbering toward him.

"Trevor!" she screamed.

He instantly recognized the terror in her voice and didn't bother stopping to look at what she was seeing. He fell back into the bedroom, turned, and slammed the window shut just as Gunther came into view.

He stared at the hideous, grotesque man looking back at him. He had to have been a foot taller than Trevor at least, and almost twice as thick. His face was twisted and deformed, just like his grandmother had wrote about, but no words could have prepared him for what he was seeing.

Gunther's left eye was gone and his left nostril was closed shut. His entire face looked like melted cheese clinging to a piece of bread, with breaks in the skin that made him think of pepperoni pizza. The man had no lips, or if he did, they were burned beyond recognition, and his mouth was bent in a way no mouth should be. Diagonally, almost, like someone had taken it and shoved the right side up as far as it would go, and the left side down.

Rain pelted his face and Trevor heard Sarah up on the roof, scrambling about to find a cellphone signal.

So did Gunther.

He looked up and then back at Trevor, his one good eye narrowing into a slit.

Then as quickly as he appeared, he was gone, and Trevor dared not stick his head out the window to find out where he went. Sarah was on her own, and he hated himself for letting her go.

He ran back to the living room where Amy was still seated on the couch. Thank God she hadn't seen Gunther, or else she truly would have gone off the deep end, never to come up for air. At least now she seemed coherent enough to understand him, and he didn't want to lose that.

"Sarah, hurry!" he shouted at the ceiling.

Up on the roof Sarah stomped her foot down hard three times, indicating she heard him. The cellphone was clutched tight in her hand and she wandered back and forth, trying to get at least one steady bar so she could make the call that would end this madness and save all of their lives.

The rain fell all around her, hard now, and she had to be careful where she stepped.

Something fell on the roof to her right, startling her. She screamed and got her footing in place before it was too late and she toppled off and to the ground below. Though she doubted the fall would kill her, it would certainly do some damage. Maybe even break a bone, and what then?

She didn't want to think about it.

She approached the object and saw it was Kincaid's severed head. She choked back her own vomit and looked over the edge of the roof. Gunther was there, staring up at her.

"Fuck you!" she screamed again.

She moved left, and so did he. She moved right, and he followed.

"Dammit."

She wanted to just focus on finding a signal but now she had more important things to worry about. Like staying alive.

She stepped back so she could no longer see him, and momentarily froze, waiting for the other shoe to drop.

It did.

She heard something being dragged across the porch and fear overtook her. What seemed like a good idea at first was now just a nightmare as she was trapped with no place to go. She took a chance and crept closer to the edge and saw him, dragging one of the deck chairs over to the front of the cabin. If he stood on it, he was tall enough so he could hoist himself up on the roof.

"Fuck."

She hammered her foot on the roof, not knowing what Trevor or Amy could do about it, but hoping nonetheless they could come up with something, and fast.

Trevor heard her cries for help and ran to kitchen. He looked out the window and saw Gunther there on the porch, stepping onto the chair.

"Sarah!" he shouted. "He's coming!"

Gunther glanced at him and Trevor stumbled back against the counter.

He looked around for something—anything—that would provide him with some help, but there was no hope. He fell to his knees on the kitchen floor and could think about nothing else but Sarah, trapped up on the roof with that...thing.

After a moment he felt a warm, shaking hand on his shoulder and Amy crouched down next to him, cradling his head against her.

"She'll be okay," she whispered.

The guilt of it all was too much for him to handle. He should have never let her go out there alone. How did it come to this? Him inside, safe for now, and his girlfriend—the woman he was supposed to do anything for—on the outside being chased by the man his grandmother once called a friend?

He sobbed uncontrollably, his body convulsing in Amy's arms.

Amy.

She was supposed to be the crazy one, not him. He had held it together for all of their sakes but now he felt like the rope was breaking. Each little string snapping loose one by one.

Be a man, his father's voice rang in his ear. *Get up and be a man.*

He couldn't. He was done for.

There was nothing left in him but fear and regret.

Sarah stomped her foot once more, but he barely heard it through the pulse-pounding headache he now had.

"Come on, Trevor. Do something," she shouted.

Gunther grabbed the roof with one hand, and then the other. Just like she had done.

She watched as the hulk of a man burrowed himself up and onto solid ground just feet away from her. She lifted the cellphone again and looked for a signal, but there was none, and she knew there never would be.

This was a bad idea.

She chucked the object at his chest just as he rose to his feet, blocking out the clouds. He approached her like she was nothing more than a mouse to be toyed with and she backed away as much as she could before reaching the opposite side of the roof.

He continued toward her.

That was it. She was going to die. Her heart pounded at the realization and she grabbed handfuls of her hair and tried to pull it free, crying and screaming like a woman possessed. She tore at her shirt and it ripped in the front, exposing her breasts to him. Rain pelted her skin and soaked her to the bone.

She glanced at the edge of the roof to her left and a small flame of optimism began burning at the tip of her head like the wick on a candle. It worked its way down through her chest, past her stomach, through her legs and into her feet, causing her to tremble with excitement, though she was still scared to death of the beast coming closer.

And closer.

And closer.

Gunther's eyes flashed to her shoes as her feet pointed left and he tried to force himself upon her but it was too late.

He charged and she ran, dashing out of the way and taking one giant leap for safety, hoping like hell she was able to propel herself far enough off of the roof so she landed in the lake to break her fall.

Gunther tried to stop his forward momentum but the rain was too much, making the roof as slippery as a used car salesman. He went sliding off of it, toppling his full weight to the ground below where he landed with a thud and stopped moving.

Sarah soared through the air and heard nothing but the beating of her own heart as her life flashed before her eyes.

So this is what death was like.

Her foot had slipped at the last moment when she jumped causing her to cry out in shame and anger.

Yet she saw it. The lake. Beneath her then as she fell toward it. Only there was something else underneath her other than clear water and sand. Something hard and unmoving.

Deer antlers.

"Oh shit."

Trevor and Amy heard the commotion on the roof and rushed to the living room window in time to see Sarah take her final swan song off of it. He watched helplessly as she fell into the water, impaling herself on the antlers of the dead deer he and Kincaid had tossed into the lake what seemed like a lifetime ago.

His hands slammed against the window, shaking the glass, and he screamed. Watching her lifeless body swaying back and forth face down in the shallow water. The antlers protruding up through her neck and back.

Amy looked away and threw up. Now she had lost two friends.

Trevor pushed his face up against the glass and slowly slid down it, causing it to squeak against his flesh.

And in his slow descent into madness, Trevor's bladder let loose and he pissed himself.

TWELVE

The stench in the cabin was almost unbearable. Between her vomit and Trevor's urine, Amy didn't know which was worse.

She watched as he fell to the ground and backed away from him, knowing there was nothing she could do to help. She had been there before already, but watching her friend Sarah die was enough of a shock to bring her back to reality and say, "Hey, I better do something or else I'm going to end up like her."

Only she didn't know what to do.

No phone, no vehicle, and no Kincaid. He was gone, just like Sarah was, leaving only her and Trevor to fend for themselves.

She looked around the cabin bathed in the soft glow of candlelight, and picked up one of the knives Trevor had brought into the living room earlier. It felt heavy in her hand. Cold. She didn't know if she had the strength to do anything with it or not, but she had to try. At least give the appearance that she was tough.

She picked up another one and slid it through her belt, which was pressed tight around her waist. The knife held and she nodded, doing the same on the other side. They caused her to maneuver in an awkward fashion at first, like she had just spent the last week riding horseback, but eventually she found the proper footing and moved faster and quicker through the cabin. Her mind somersaulted as she tried to figure out what to do next.

Trevor whimpered in the living room and managed to bring himself back to his knees so he could stare out the window again at Sarah's corpse.

Amy came up behind him and tried to tear him away from the macabre view but he shoved her off and she fell over the coffee table, nearly impaling herself on one of the knives she had fastened securely against herself.

She withdrew the two blades from her belt and tossed them to the ground, thinking twice about having them that close to her.

She glared at Trevor, feeling sorry for him, and shook her head. She could have been angry—should have been angry—but she wasn't. He was in so much pain now and there was nothing she could do. She would just have to hope he could snap himself out of it in time to save his own, like she had done.

Because that time was coming sooner rather than later.

A thud outside against the far, living room wall, told her so.

She picked up one of the journals and aimlessly flipped through it, not knowing what she was doing. Words like madman, psycho, terror, and savage penetrated her brain while she flipped through the pages and thought about how awful it must have been for Trevor's grandmother to have to go through all of that.

But it was nothing compared to what they were experiencing now.

She threw the book on the ground and went into the kitchen. Amy had to keep moving because she knew if she stopped it would all sink in again and she would collapse in a crumpled heap on the floor, just like Trevor.

She opened and closed the fridge, and saw a shadow move across the kitchen window. She couldn't tell if it was Gunther or a tree swaying in the breeze brought on by the storm, but either way it startled her and she screamed. It felt good to be making noise again, even if that noise was caused by outright fear.

When she was in her catatonic state a million different things ran through her mind. Surviving, dying, but most of all she kept seeing Kincaid's head and his dead eyes staring up at her from the cabin's porch. He had been such a sweet guy to her over the years, even when they weren't a couple. Always making sure she was taken care of, doing his best to comfort her when she was feeling down, and sharing in the good times she experienced growing up.

Now he was gone, and she'd never, ever, kiss his lips again.

She closed her eyes tight and shook the thoughts away like a dog shaking off water. She couldn't think about that anymore. Not now. Maybe when it was all was over she could grieve properly, but first she had to survive.

Trevor wailed in front of the living room window and all she could do was go and console him as best she could, hoping this time he wouldn't throw her away like used tissue.

"Trevor?" she whispered.

She saw nothing but the back of his head, but when she looked closer she could see his face mirrored in the glass of the window. His eyes were wild and crazy. Unflinching and wide.

"Trevor?" she asked again, this time approaching him with care.

He slowly turned his face to her and she gasped.

Every ounce of color had drained from it to the point where he looked like a vampire. The circles under his eyes were dark and pronounced and his lip curled up into a sadistic grin she had only ever seen on the face of serial killers in those documentaries her father liked to watch on Netflix from time to time.

Amy backed away from him as he got to his feet, clutching the windowsill for dear life. He stood hunched over, swaying like a gentle breeze.

Was that it? The end of him?

He licked his lips and moved his jaw up and down like he was trying to say something; only his voice was too quiet and raspy for her to make out any coherent sounds. Taking a chance, she leaned in closer to him, never releasing her eyes from his.

"I'm…to…him."

Amy cocked her head to the side, puzzled.

"Say it again," she pleaded.

He snickered, snarled like a wild animal, and this time spoke louder so there would be no mistaking his intentions.

"I'm going to kill him."

Amy backed away, clutching the knife in her hand for dear life.

"Trevor. No," she whispered.

He looked at the overturned coffee table and saw the revolver on the floor. Amy had a chance to glance at the object but before she could do or say anything else, he snatched it off the ground in flash and bolted for the cabin's front door.

"Trevor!" she screamed after him, but it was useless.

She ran after him and watched as he threw open the door and went out into the night. A flash of lightning illuminated his body and Amy slammed it shut, bolting it locked behind him.

There was nothing else she could do.

THIRTEEN

Trevor heard Amy call after him but didn't care.

His fingers gripped the handle of the revolver as tight as humanly possible and he went around the side of the cabin to where he had seen Gunther when he was first hoisting Sarah up onto the roof. By the bedroom.

Spots came and went before his eyes and he tried to blink them away but they remained, flashing on and off like a strobe light. His mind was lost and all he could think about was getting revenge for Sarah's death. He no longer cared about himself, or Amy.

All he wanted to do was kill.

His feet sloshed through the mud and grass and Trevor approached the window. He saw the deep indents of Gunther's footprints, but no Gunther. He sniffed the air like a wild beast.

Takes one to know one, he thought.

He went around to the far side of the cabin, rounding the corner without even thinking about his own safety. If the savage was there, then he was there, and Trevor would put a bullet in his skull.

But there was no one there.

Trevor looked up at the roof, thinking he'd see the crazed man staring down at him, but again. Nothing.

Another flash of lightning lit up the area around him and he saw muddy footprints leading around the other side of the cabin. The side the deck was on. Sure enough, when he rounded that corner, he saw them trailing back to the front of the cabin.

He also saw Sarah's body lying in the water, being pounded with rain.

Trevor approached her with care and gingerly crouched down on his knees, wanting nothing more than to reach out and touch her one last time, but he couldn't. If he did he would risk slipping and falling into the water himself and what then? The gun would be soaked and useless, and he'd find himself in a whole new world of hurt next to his dead girlfriend.

Dead girlfriend.

The words rang in his ears like an alarm bell and he shut his eyes tight, trying to stave off the sound. He clutched his temples for a moment and then his eyes snapped open. He saw through Sarah. Through her lifeless corpse and to her heart. The heart that had been so good to him through the years. Always believing in him, that he could do anything with his life if he just put his mind to it.

"For you, baby," he whispered.

A pounding behind him diverted his attention and he got to his feet and spun around to see Amy at the living room window, banging away on it and screaming, but a roaring clap of thunder prevented him from understanding what she was saying.

She looked to her right and started pointing with a thin, trembling finger.

Trevor turned as yet another flicker of lightning revealed Gunther, standing not more than ten feet away from him.

He was huge. Much bigger than Trevor had first thought, and he began to shiver with rage at what this madman had done to Sarah.

The lightning dissipated, shielding him once again in the shadows but Trevor would never forget that face. It was etched in his mind like a radiation burn. He would take it with him to the grave and beyond.

"Not today," he said, and raised the revolver.

The candlelight from the living room shone across his cheek, casting him in an eerie orange glow. He licked his lips and cocked the hammer. The cylinder turned.

Gunther never moved.

Trevor shut one eye, aimed for the chest, and fired.

A loud crack penetrated the sound of the rain scattering all around them.

A look of shock crossed his face. He did it, and couldn't believe it. He had won. The beast was vanquished and he had his revenge for Sarah. He screamed and waited for the savage to fall.

Gunther never moved.

Trevor glanced at Amy, whose eyes were also wide with shock. She shook her head.

What the hell?

Trevor raised the gun and fired again.

And again.

And again.

Gunther never moved.

A sick feeling rose in Trevor's stomach as he emptied the revolver, firing two more shots he swore connected with the brute in front of him. How could they not? He was huge, and a hard target to miss. Trevor had never fired a gun before in his life but he knew enough to point and shoot and watch whatever you were aiming at fall.

But it never went that way.

The knife at Gunther's side rose slowly and Trevor shouted into the night, turning the revolver over in his hands. He wiped the barrel free of water droplets. There were markings on it. Light indentations etched into the steel no one had noticed before because it had been covered in dirt and dust.

PROPERTY OF HUNTSVILLE THEATER.

"A fucking prop?"

His mind reeled at the revelation and spun back to yesterday when he was sitting on the couch reading from his grandmother's journals. She made mention of her time in the theater but he didn't clue in until that moment.

She had saved a prop from her glory days, and the bullets were nothing but blanks.

"Fuck me," Trevor said.

Gunther advanced on him but rather than run, Trevor dropped the fake revolver to the ground and raised his eyes to meet his maker. There was no point in running any longer.

He had nothing left to live for.

Amy screamed and pounded the glass, watching as her last remaining friend stood there and did nothing while Gunther raised his blade and brought it down with as much force as he could, embedding it in Trevor's skull.

His body trembled and shook. The knife cutting halfway through his face and stopping just above his nose.

Blood ran down his chin and chest, washing away with the rain. His carcass wanted to fall but it couldn't. The knife was securely in place, and Gunther held him up by its handle.

He looked at Amy.

A bolt of lightning struck the lake behind him and she fell back onto the floor at the sight of his deformed face.

"No," she whimpered. "Please."

Gunther's right hand took hold of Trevor's body just under the armpit and lifted it a foot off the ground. His left hand released the knife and clutched his left hip bone, swaying Trevor's body back and forth like a rag doll.

Amy saw what he meant to do and scattered out of the way of the window.

Gunther propelled Trevor through the glass, shattering it into a hundred pieces across the cabin's hardwood floor. His body soared through the air and landed with a thud on the couch on the other side of the room, rolling off of it and onto the stack of journals.

Amy screamed and crawled like a crab toward the kitchen.

Gunther lifted one leg over the windowsill, and then the other.

He was home.

FOURTEEN

Gunther looked at the carnage in the cabin and grunted. He threw the coffee table against the back wall and it shattered, creating a mess of wooden splinters and more shattered glass.

Amy kept screaming and he turned his attention to her, watching as she tried to free herself from the inevitable. He didn't know who she was or what she was doing there. All he knew was she had to die. Just like the rest.

No one could ever know he existed.

No one but Martha.

He glanced all around the cabin. So many memories came flooding back and he stopped, closing his eye and breathing deep through his one good nostril, as if he could smell Martha's perfume once again permeating the air.

It had all been okay, before the fire. Life was good with her and he could see himself living out the rest of his days by her side, even if it was only for a little while in the summer. She had let him stay at the cabin all year round, even when she wasn't there, and he loved her for it. He had no place else to go.

Before her, he was nothing.

A wanderer.

A vagabond.

She made him who he was, in more ways than one.

He opened his eye and glared at Amy, who was frozen in place on the floor, staring up at him.

Gunther towered over her and she tried to think of something, anything, to stop him from doing what he had done to the others. The knife she held in her hands seemed like nothing more than a toy now that he was in front of her. His bulky frame swaying before her eyes like a pendulum.

He came closer, his feet thumping against the floor, sending vibrations up through her spine. She quivered as tears streamed down her cheeks and dripped onto her bare arms. She shook her head, pleading with him.

"No, no, no, no."

Gunther ignored her cries and bent over her thin, fragile body. She was skinnier than the other one, and shorter. Yet she was just as pretty.

A shame.

He reached out and clutched her throat.

Amy winced as he lifted her to her feet. She uselessly batted at his tree trunk arm, crying out for him to release her. His fingers tightened their grasp on her throat and she could feel her windpipe giving way.

Her eyes scanned the cabin, searching for some way to defeat the beast.

Then, out of nowhere, her mind began repeating the same words over and over and in a last ditch effort to survive, she lied.

"I'm her granddaughter," she gasped.

Gunther's fingers stopped squeezing but didn't loosen.

She tried again, sensing she might be getting through to him.

"I'm her granddaughter," Amy wheezed again.

This time his fingers gave way and released her.

Amy fell to the ground and looked up at him with wide, frightened eyes. Fearing he would see through her ploy in a split second and smash his foot down on her skull.

He didn't.

He simply looked down on her and if he could have frowned, he would.

"I'm her granddaughter," she said again, this time more pronounced as she rubbed her throat, trying to soothe it. "Martha is my grandmother."

Gunther stumbled backward, shaking his head.

Was this true?

He knew his love had grandchildren but he had never met any of them. This girl. Was she...it couldn't be? What had he done?

Amy got to her feet and tried to think of a way to prove herself to him. She thought back to all of the things Trevor had ever told her about his grandmother, but nothing came clear in her mind.

Then she saw the journals lying on the ground and made a move toward them.

Gunther cautiously stepped to his right, blocking her way.

Amy flinched and stepped back.

She took a deep breath, knowing she was treading on very, very thin ice. One wrong move and her life would be over in an instant. She had to try, though. It was the only thing she had left.

"I want to show you," she said to him.

He cocked his head to the side. His eye blinked at her.

"I want to show you how much she loved you."

He made a sound what she could only interpret as a gasp and backed away, giving her enough room to walk past him.

Amy gingerly took one step, and then another, brushing up against the man who had killed all of her friends. His stench was overwhelming and she held her breath.

Arms trembling.

Knees weak.

He turned and watched as she bent and picked up one of the small leather books. He had no idea what could possibly in it, but she had told him she would speak of Martha's love for him, and he had to hear it one more time. Had to give her a moment to speak, and if not—if she was lying to him—he could reach out and snap her neck.

His fists opened and closed as if to prove his point, and Amy watched him closely. She prayed to whatever god was watching over her she had the right journal in her hands. One that spoke of how Martha felt about Gunther in their early days together, rather than how she had reacted to him after the fire burned him so badly, turning him into the madman he was now.

She choked back a sob and opened the book, flipping through the pages. Scanning them.

He stepped toward her and she held out her hand.

"Here. Right here," she said, letting out an exasperated sigh of relief.

Gunther stopped moving and waited.

"June 14th," she began. "I have never been so happy as I am now. Gunther makes me feel alive every time I lay my eyes upon him. It's as if I have been born again into this world and am experiencing everything for the first time. So fresh and new. Colors so bright. Air so clean. Sounds so loud they fill my heart with so much joy I feel it might burst with happiness."

Gunther's knees felt weak for the first time in a long time and he braced himself against the cabin wall. It was true. How could this girl know about these books if she was not Martha's granddaughter?

Amy eyes flickered over him and she felt a surge of hope swell up in her heart. Maybe she'd make it out of this after all.

She kept reading.

"We spent the day together under the sun, basking in all its glory. Its rays warming my heart as much as this man who has come into my life. His strong hands make me feel safe but when he touches me, it's as soft as a butterfly's wing. His kiss is delicate, his skin is tender, and I cannot imagine myself ever loving another man as much as I love Gunther."

She pronounced his name slowly, as if to hammer home the point she was trying to make.

Gunther.

That was him.

His good eye clouded over with emotion. Emotions he had not felt in a long, long time. Even when Martha was around. How could he have been so foolish? Treating her, and life, with such disdain when all she wanted was for him to love her and make her feel like the woman she deserved to be.

Sweet, sweet Martha.

He sunk down against the wall and Amy began crying. No longer because she was afraid, but because she knew everything was going to be okay. Her words had gotten through to him. Trevor's grandmother's words. The words she had left behind for someone to find. Possibly Gunther himself.

There was only one thing left to do.

She glanced over his shoulder at the kitchen where one of his hunting knives still sat in the sink, rinsing.

Amy closed the journal but Gunther put out his hand. Reaching toward her and twiddling his fingers for her to keep going.

It was all he had left.

Amy's chest heaved and she opened the journal once more, reading from it slowly while approaching him.

She spoke more of Martha's love for him, and how happy he made her. All the while glancing at the kitchen, thinking about the knife and how much strength it would take to impale it into his neck.

She was just inches away from him now, and Amy crouched down and placed a hand on his shoulder while continuing to read. Telling him in Martha's own words as best she could how she loved him more than life itself and wanted to be with him forever.

Gunther sobbed and placed his head on her shoulder.

She trembled at his touch but knew it would all be over soon.

All she had to do was keep him grounded and get to the knife.

"I love him," she said again and again. "I love him, I love him, I love him."

She wrapped her arm around his neck and held the madman tight against her while he cried. Never did she think it would come to this. It should have all ended with them alive, driving far away from the cabin in Trevor's minivan. Going back home to their parents and lives, living out their days with one another. Laughing and sharing in each other's experiences even if they lost touch, as friends so often do.

Amy closed the journal and dropped it between them, soothing him with soft hushes while rubbing his massive back as if he were a child.

She wasn't sure how long she stayed like that with but after a while she took a chance and whispered in his ear, hoping he would be able to understand her.

"I'm going to get us some water," she said.

Gunther clutched her arm tighter for a moment but eventually gave up, nodding that it was okay for her to move.

He wouldn't harm her.

"Thank you," she whispered, and stood up.

She walked slowly toward the kitchen, glancing over her shoulder to make sure the big man was still resting comfortably on the ground.

He was.

She reached into the cupboard and pulled out a glass and ran the faucet, rinsing it out perhaps a little longer than she should have while her free hand gripped one of the hunting knives tight and pulled it out of the sink.

Amy filled the glass with water and looked over her shoulder once more.

Gunther was still on the floor.

His shoulders rising and falling with each deep breath he took.

She shut off the running water and turned quick, keeping the knife concealed behind her back while holding the glass in front of her.

It was what survival was all about. Doing anything it took to stay alive and living to see another day.

Even if it meant lying.

She approached Gunther from behind and leaned over to see him flipping through the journal she had dropped at his feet.

Her heart leaped into her throat and the glass of water shook in her hand, the cool liquid spilling out over her knuckles.

She didn't just lie about being Martha's granddaughter. She had lied about the contents of the journal.

It was one of the books describing how insane Gunther had become, and how she had been afraid for her life in his very presence. In a last ditch effort to save herself, Amy had pretended to read something that wasn't there. Thinking back to the other entries Trevor had read the day before, trying to capture the same voice his grandmother had written them in.

She croaked her fear and dropped the glass to the floor. It shattered, sending water spilling out and around her feet, seeping toward Gunther.

His head snapped to the side as he realized the truth.

Amy did all she could and brought the knife out from behind her back. She raised it high over hear head, thanking the stars the side of his face without any vision was turned toward her, and with everything she had left in her she thrust the blade down with as much force as she could, impaling it in the side of his neck, sending it cutting through tendons and muscle until it was buried deep in his body.

She released the handle and stepped back as he rose from the ground, screaming and twirling around and around, crashing into the cabin walls, nearly putting himself through them.

He reached out for her but Amy backed away further.

Toward the front door.

Gunther wailed and broke everything in sight, furious with the girl who had lied to him. She was no more Martha's granddaughter than he was. He should have known it wasn't true. Martha hated him and everything he had become, but he couldn't stop himself. Not now. Not ever. He would go on living out his days there at the cabin. Alone.

Angry.

He just had one last thing to do.

Gunther stepped forward once more but this time found his knees wobbling underneath him.

Amy watch as he faltered, swaying left to right, and looked at the knife still impaled deep within him. She was amazed he had managed to stay alive so long.

He knocked some candles over and they toppled to the ground, their flames still burning.

Catching the living room curtains that had fallen off their pole when he had thrown Trevor through the window.

Gunther looked back over his shoulder, continuing to wobble, and fell to his knees.

Fire.

Pain.

He lifted his head high toward the ceiling and screamed.

Amy watched him react to the flames beginning to engulf the cabin.

She quickly got her wits about her and picked up a bottle of tequila from the kitchen counter and threw it at the savage. It shattered in front of him, sending shards of glass and alcohol up and onto his chest and neck.

Gunther batted at the liquid dripping off of him and looked at Amy. He wanted to catch her. Wanted to take her in his hands and snap her in half, but he was frozen. His neck and shoulder ached beyond belief and every twitch, every movement brought him more pain and suffering.

Amy, sensing he would like to tear her apart, did the only thing she could think of. She scrambled around in one of the kitchen drawers until she found a book of matches.

She lit one and it quickly extinguished itself.

Then she tried another, and another, and another.

Frustrated, she screamed and cried, knowing she was doing herself a disservice, but unable to help the fear and hope mixing within her like a cocktail.

If she could just light one match.

Just one.

She struck the phosphorous head of the last one in the pack against the course line running across the bottom of it.

The flame flickered and grew.

Amy's eyes widened as she stared into it, hypnotized for a moment at its beauty.

Fire.

The source of all life.

And death.

She took a couple of steps toward Gunther and threw the fiery stick at him. He tried to bat it away before it made contact but it struck his chest and instantly the alcohol soaking his torn and ragged shirt went up in flames.

He howled and Amy didn't stick around to see the result of her attack. She spun and ran toward the front door, throwing it open and bolting into the night as quick as she could.

As quick as the fire was spreading inside the cabin.

FIFTEEN

She fell deeper into the woods without knowing it before finally stopping to catch a breath.

Amy placed her hands on her knees and doubled over, barely able to contain the sickness in her stomach. She looked back over her shoulder and saw the smoke rising high into the air, and a bright orange glow illuminating the treetops and beyond.

The cabin was engulfed in flames.

She thought about going back, but only for a moment.

Images of Gunther reeling and lumbering toward her stuck in her mind, and after a few more moments rest, she continued running.

She ran as fast and as hard as she could, with no destination in mind. She knew she just had to get away.

Get away from the pain, the horror, and the sadness. Run until she was a different person. Someone who could forget about the images she had seen tonight.

Trevor dead and lying on the cabin floor. His corpse left to burn.

Sarah impaled on the very deer antlers they had demanded Kincaid and Trevor get rid of.

Her boyfriend's severed head lying on the ground at her feet. Staring up at her.

She wanted to forget all of those things. Become someone whose memories were happy and peaceful, but the more Amy ran, the more she remembered.

Things would never be the same again and no matter where she ended up, she would never forget.

That night was etched into her mind for all eternity. She only hoped when death finally caught up with her it would take pity on her and make her whole again, for she had lost a piece of herself.

A piece of her innocence.

She stumbled over a large rock stuck in the ground and fell to her knees. The skin tore and blood oozed out from the wound, but as quickly and as suddenly as she fell, Amy got back up and kept going.

She would always keep going.

SIXTEEN

The smoldering remains of the cabin sizzled as the fire crew packed up their hoses and the Marshall walked his way through the rubble.

Police and ambulance crews were on hand to tend to the surviving victims of this horrible tragedy, but none remained alive for them to bandage or rush to a nearby hospital so they stood around, scratching their heads and writing reports, trying to make sense of it all.

Officer Grant Waldorf sat against the hood of his cruiser, eyeballing the minivan and listening as a set of tires crunched dirt and rock, approaching what was left of the cabin. He quickly set down the travel mug full of coffee he had poured himself that morning, which was now bitter cold, and turned to face the vehicle entering the scene.

Overhead the noonday sun beat down on him.

He removed his cap and wiped the sweat off of his forehead, just as the occupants stepped out of the light blue Saturn.

A man and a woman. Older. Their faces sullen and frightened all at once.

The man was cradling the woman in his arms.

"Oh shit." He snapped his fingers at his fellow officer, Brian Grady. "Hold them back," he said.

Grant rushed to help him as Trevor's mother looked upon what was left of her dead mothers' cabin. She tried to make a run for it. She had to know what was left of her baby boy, if anything. Her husband struggled to hold her back but she screamed and battered him hard against the chest.

Officers Waldorf and Grady joined him, pleading with her to calm down.

It would be okay, they told her.

She fell to her knees in the dirt and mud, soiling her slacks. Clawing at her cheeks and wailing so loud that a murder of crows sitting watchful in the trees above scattered into the sky, casting shadows over top of them as they passed in front of the sun looking for quieter pasture.

It would never be okay again.

A year later, when all was said and done and everyone had moved on with their lives, Trevor's mother sat in her kitchen with her hands wrapped around a hot cup of tea, thinking back to that day.

The telephone rang and she shook, startled. Snapping back to reality.

She listened as her husband spoke in soft whispers in the other room, watching him pace back and forth. Disappearing and reappearing in front of the archway that led from the kitchen to the living room.

Even before he got off the phone she knew the outcome of his conversation. She had been waiting for it.

They both had.

He hung up the telephone and came in to see her sitting there, looking up at him. Eyes hopeful.

"We sold it," he said quietly.

She nodded and took a sip of her tea.

"Who?" she asked.

He reached into his pocket and pulled out a scrap of paper.

"The Marchand family."

He sat down next to her and took his wife by the hand.

The ground their son had perished on was theirs no longer, and they both cried.

Four hours away the land on which the cabin once stood sat quiet. Patches of grass littered the dead soil and Whisper Lake sloshed against the bank as a deer scampered across the ravaged area.

All around it the woods stood watching.

Waiting in silence.

Breathing.

ABOUT THE AUTHOR

James Melzer is an award-winning novelist and short story writer. Since branching out on his own to become a self-published author in 2011, Melzer has sold more than half-a-million eBooks around the globe in various genres including horror, erotica, romance, crime, humor, and many others.

Whisper Lake is his first book in print.

He currently resides in Pennsylvania with his wife, stepdaughter, and husky.

www.jamesmelzer.net